The Lady and The Captain

Book 2
Gentlemen of Honor Series

by

Beverly Adam

www.lachesispublishing.com

Published Internationally by Lachesis Publishing Inc.
Rockland, Ontario
Copyright © 2013 Beverly Adam
Exclusive cover © Laura Givens
Inside artwork © 2013 Giovanna Lagana

A catalogue record for the print format of this title is available
from the National Library of Canada

ISBN 978-1-927555-31-6

A catalogue record for the Ebook is available
from the National Library of Canada
Ebooks are available for purchase from
www.lachesispublishing.com

ISBN 978-1-927555-30-9

Editor: Joanna D'Angelo

Copyeditor: Giovanna Lagana

Dedication

For my children Natasha and Julian,
and to my dearest friend, Major Hye-Kyoung Kim,
with love.

Acknowledgments

My thanks to the team at Lachesis Publishing.
You have polished this tale into a real gem.

Also Available

The Spinster and the Earl

Coming Soon

The Widow and the Rogue

The Lady and The Captain

Chapter 1

West Coast of Ireland—Varrik Island

Rain battered against the glass pane of the cottage window. Sarah Clogheen drew the heavy woolen curtains to prevent the damp cold from seeping in. She shivered and wrapped her shawl more closely about her, then set another piece of turf onto the fire. She was Irish, born and raised, and yet she could never get used to her country's temperamental weather. As the turf sparked into a warming flame, she heard an unexpected pounding on the front door. A dark silhouette framed the window, but with the rain pelting down, it was difficult to tell who it could be.

Perhaps a lost sailor seeking shelter from the storm? Or another one of those religious zealots come to trouble them? One of those interfering simpletons who foolishly believed that the reclusive wise women were practicing black magic instead of the healing arts. Frowning with concern, she wondered if she should open the door. But what if it was someone in need? A stranded sailor whose ship had gone off course because of the storm?

She sighed, putting down the heavy poker. As a wise woman, she was obligated to help all who came to her door. It didn't matter who stood there. Priest or pirate, she would offer them hospitality. She could not go on and blithely ignore them

Slowly, she pulled back the latch—

A heavy gust of wind swept into the room, sending everything a-flutter. She looked out into the darkness and was greeted by the sight of a man standing on her doorstep.

The stranger stood slightly stooped over, his left shoulder leaning tiredly against the doorframe. To add to his unexpected appearance was the astonishing fact that he was carrying another man on his back.

Sarah's cornflower blue eyes opened wide in surprise.

The cottage was located on a steep hill. Yet this stranger had somehow managed to carry a grown man all the way up. It was a feat never done before. Most of the ill brought to the island were either left on the beach in a lean-to or carried in a handcart manned by several relatives.

Faith, she thought, this stranger certainly is no feeble fop. Here is a man who by mere action demands my respect.

She quickly noted that he was a few years older than her and had a head of thick, black hair. She thought him to be somewhere in his late twenties. There was another unsettling fact to their presence. They were both ranking naval officers, as evidenced by their fitted dark blue wool uniforms, undoubtedly from an English warship located somewhere nearby. But before she could ask any questions, she noticed the standing officer wince. His grip was loosening. The heavy body of the pale-faced man he carried slid down one side of his back.

A quick glance at the other officer and she knew by the twin gold epaulets attached to his coat that he was a captain. More unsettling than this observation was the obvious reason for their unannounced visit. The gentleman was gravely ill. He was, if she could discern by the pallor of his face, on the verge of complete collapse. This was not going to be a simple matter of offering shelter from the storm.

It was evident why the English stranger came to her door in the middle of a tempest. He and his companion were seeking help. Her skills as a wise woman were once more about to be put to the test.

*　*　*

"Who are you?" she asked.

Lieutenant Robert Smythe had seen many beautiful women in his life, but this young woman left him speechless. His dark brown eyes widened in an open stare. Clearly, she wasn't disconcerted by his reaction. *She must leave everyone she meets in awe at her beauty.*

For a witch, as the wise woman was considered by the superstitious, she was an unexpectedly becoming one. Her light blue eyes and shiny hair, the shade of a glowing halo, gave her an almost angelic appearance. She was not the ruddy-faced wise woman one typically saw by a sick bed. She was something else entirely . . . lovely and alluring.

A brisk wind whipped around her long layers of skirts, molding the dark wool against her shapely legs. He caught a scent of lavender and sage from her clothes. It reminded him of a field of wildflowers.

Belatedly, he realized she was staring up at him expectantly.

"I'm Lieutenant Robert Smythe of his majesty's warship, The Brunswick," he said, at last finding his voice. "And this is Captain Jackson," he gestured towards the sick man. Not wearing a cap, he saluted her with two fingers to his forehead.

"I've come to ask the help of the healer, Gladys Clogheen of Varrik-on-Suir. May we enter?"

"I am Sarah. Gladys Clogheen is my mother. Come in," she said and gestured them inside.

He carried the ill captain into the main room. Pushing against the wind, Sarah bolted the door behind them. She pointed to an empty lounge chair located next to the fire. Gently, he lay the sick captain down.

Smoldering peat bricks scented the air. Robert made as if to speak, to ask a question, but she held a finger to her lips silencing him. Her full attention was now upon her new patient, the ailing captain. Immediately, she began to examine him. Holding the ill man's wrist, she checked his pulse. It was erratic. Occasionally, she nodded, counting softly in a strange tongue. She uttered foreign words that he couldn't follow. He frowned slightly. It was the first time he'd ever heard Irish spoken.

He had some smattering acquaintance with Portuguese, Spanish, and French. But this Celtic tongue was new to his ears. The native language of the region was seldom heard outside of the western and more remote regions of Ireland.

The English had almost successfully conquered the people and language of Ireland, supplanting their language with their own. But the Irish people well understood the old saying that went, "A country without a language is a country without its soul."

Stubbornly thumbing their noses at their invaders, the Irish continued to secretly use their language and practice their unique music. This they did despite threats and deprivations. Here on the southern part of the Emerald Isles, they lived beyond The Pale, the invisible dividing line separating Irish-speaking Ireland from the English speaking.

The officer mentally shrugged off any uneasiness he may have normally felt about hearing the ancient language. As an officer in his majesty's service, he ought to have been appalled at the wise woman using the forbidden tongue. Astonishingly, he did not.

The way the woman spoke made the foreign language sound musical to his ears. There was a serenity

[14]

in her voice—both soothing and natural. She had a self-assurance about her steady manners that inspired confidence. Clearly, her mother had taught her the healing arts, as well.

Robert watched her open the captain's long overcoat, and loosen his shirt. Putting an ear against his chest, she listened more closely to his unsteady heart. Lastly, she examined his tongue, prying open the officer's mouth. Robert made a brusque gesture. He silently protested at this final intrusion of his captain's private person. She had no right to touch him this way.

The wise woman waved a hand, effectively warding him off. "You're interfering, Lieutenant," she said, a note of stern displeasure in her voice. "I need to see how your captain's insides are faring. So kindly do us both a grand favor and stay out of my way. If ye can't abide seeing me touching him, I suggest you go outside and cool off in the rain and think about why you came here."

He said no more. Silently, he acknowledged her authority. Keeping his tongue in his head, he continued to observe her, wondering what made such an innocent and lovely young woman such as this take on the very challenging and quite intimate work of a healer.

Moving her hand gently over the semiconscious man, Sarah tried to detect where he felt the most discomfort. By the painful tightening of his face, she discerned his innards were causing him the sharpest pangs of agony. Cramps, no doubt, were making it painful there, she noted. This was no ordinary case of indigestion. Something far more sinister was at work.

Restless and full of deliriums, Captain Jackson sat up. The chaise lounge creaked with the abrupt movement. He reached his hands out and shouted frantically, "Pull that sail tighter, lads! Tie that rigging you bit of yellow-bellied shark bait before she tears. The devil take it. What are you standing around here for, boy? Get below to where you belong! Blithering fool. Move your carcass out of the boom's way before you end up in the dink."

Sarah and Robert exchanged concerned glances as Captain Jackson thrashed about.

"Man overboard!" He made a gesture as if he were throwing a rope to a drowning man, grasping at the air in a hand-over-hand gesture, pulling on the invisible rope as he tossed and turned in his fevered delirium.

Sarah looked into his glazed eyes. They were wide open. Captain Jackson acted as if she wasn't there. He was oblivious to her presence. Shaking her head, she started to mumble a few words that Robert could barely make out.

"*Musha, musha*, what have they done to ye? How did ye come to be like this? Poor wretched man . . . what's to be done?"

Abruptly, she stood up and left his side.

*   *   *

Robert watched Sarah enter a curtained-off part of the cottage on the opposite side of the large hearth. Behind the curtain was a bed. Robert could see an older woman, propped up by several large pillows. The lady was about the captain's age, in her mid-forties. The woman's wavy black hair was streaked with gray and modestly pulled back under a white lace cap. He realized that she must be the wise woman, Gladys Clogheen.

Her face was strangely wise and noble with high cheekbones and a serene expression in her eyes. Those light honey-colored eyes were assessing Robert now, as if weighing his person against what the blonde angel was telling her in Irish. He could discern that this seemingly frail woman had some power over the young healer.

The young, wise woman listened respectfully to her as the ailing healer spoke in gasping breaths. She softly responded in kind to her questions. The older woman nodded in agreement to whatever was being discussed. At last they finished their conversation. The blonde woman gave the frail, older woman a gentle squeeze of her hand and tucked her back into bed.

There was no doubt there was a strong bond between the two. And assuredly the older, wise woman had been consulted about Captain Jackson's condition. Robert wondered what had been decided. Could these women heal Captain Jackson of this mysterious malady? Or was his commander doomed to certain death?

*   *   *

Sarah returned to the hearth and gestured for him to come closer. Her face was grave. The news she had to impart was not good.

"Well?" he asked.

"How has the captain been faring before now? Has he complained of stomach cramps and other digestive ailments? What of the other men aboard, did any of the hands suffer from similar complaints as his?"

"Aye, Captain Jackson complained of cramps. He has also experienced a loss of sensitivity in his limbs and he's been having trouble with his hearing of late. But those difficulties would come and go, until this . . . ," he answered honestly. "He became deathly ill nigh on two days ago. It was then I decided to seek your help. Many of my men had heard of your mother's renowned skills as a wise woman and recommended her to me."

She nodded at this remark.

Indeed their reputation as healers had spread all the way to the English navy. Aye, there had been many a desperate sailor who'd come to them in hopes of being healed from ailments that appeared to be hopelessly incurable. But she knew for this proud English lieutenant to have sought her help meant she was his last hope. She saw fear in his dark eyes. She sensed he was afraid his captain would die.

Sarah continued with her questioning. There were too many unknowns and she had to eliminate every other possible illness before she could get to the right one.

"Were your provisions fresh when the captain began to take ill?"

"Yes, they were, but if you are about to suggest that our provisions were in any manner compromised," he replied, "I must disagree. None of the other men aboard have suffered any similar complaints. Therefore, I do not believe our water or spirits have been in any way tainted." As a result, he hadn't asked the Admiralty to launch a board of inquiry and send inspectors to assess the ship. Nor did he intend to do so when it returned to England, he silently promised himself.

Sarah made no comment about Robert's remark that the food was untainted. Instead, she continued her inquiry. She had a list of questions. This was not going to be an easy diagnosis.

"How long ago was the last time you noted these difficulties with the captain's limbs?"

"That would be about nigh on seven days ago."

"And his meals are served with the rest of the crew's?"

He shook his head.

"Nay . . . he's the highest ranking officer aboard and like other captains has his mess fixed for him by his own steward."

She gave him a quizzical look, her brow furrowed in thought.

"He has a servant fix his meals, Lieutenant? Was it

separate from the rest of the men's mess? Did he consume food different from them?"

"Aye, it is a common enough practice. If an officer wishes, he can purchase his own rations and have them prepared by his own servants. Now that Captain Jackson has become well off, it would have been tightfisted of him not to use some of his winnings. He uses his blunt for his own comfort and that of those who serve beneath him. He can well afford it."

He smiled, remembering their shared victories—the moments that had sealed his friendship with Captain Jackson. The battles had also helped earn him respect from the ordinary sailors and fellow ranked officers. The smell of gunpowder, the raising of swords and bludgeoning cudgels as they stealthily climbed aboard an enemy warship in the dark of night, quickly capturing the vessel. At such moments a man could easily lose his life or gain a fortune.

It was those vivid memories that gave him reason not to abandon Captain Jackson to that worthless sawbones of a ship's surgeon who'd condemned him to his doom.

"I will not abandon him now," he said, a glint of determination in his eyes. "I will do everything in my power to save him."

She took careful note of his resolve. It was most commendable.

Wisely, she made no comment. She first needed to confirm what she suspected was the root cause of the mysterious illness. It was sapping the life and spirit out of the English commander.

"His servant, was he sick like Captain Jackson? Did he eat of the same food as his master?" she asked, biting down on her lower lip in thought.

"He was not ill when last seen," he said, his tone changing to one of slight impatience. "And, aye, the steward ate the captain's food, as well. The troublesome part is that I cannot be certain of anything now." He looked unsure.

"Why is that?" she asked.

"His man has gone missing."

He shook his head sadly before continuing. "It is believed the steward fell overboard in the middle of a particularly treacherous gale, like the one battering outside. He is thought to have drowned. That occurred the day before we came near these southern shores."

He remembered the storm. The gale had hit just before The Brunswick reached the southwest coast. It happened as they were descending from the north. There had been a hurried bustle of activity and a sense of urgency as the small frigate was tossed about on the rough seas.

"Our experienced able-bodied seamen were ordered to fasten down the riggings and sails. The idlers, those who were not experienced hands, were ordered to dutifully man the bilge pumps. They were set to the task of pumping the water out of the hull." He ran his fingers through his hair as he continued. "We had the very devil of a time of it that night. It was a hair-raising experience requiring all our skills at once."

Sarah nodded in understanding. She couldn't help but notice how thick and attractive his hair was as his fingers combed through it. She gazed at him for a moment, and then mentally gave herself a shake. She shouldn't be noticing such things, she told herself. The poor man needed her help. "Please continue, Lieutenant. Everything you are telling me is of importance to my diagnosis," she said in encouragement.

The lieutenant cleared his throat and added, "It was also the first time I took over full command for Captain Jackson. Aye, between fighting the gale and putting out the fire, it was pure bedlam. Among the idlers were the chief cook and his crew, as well as the captain's steward. It was in the middle of the gale that the mizzenmast went up in flames. My men reported it had been struck by lightning. At the same time, unbeknownst to anyone, Captain Jackson's steward, John Stafford, was swept away into the sea." He paused in his telling, visibly upset. "The man's disappearance went unnoticed till the next day."

"A tragedy to be sure," Sarah murmured. She could tell the event greatly troubled him. His brow was furrowed as he revealed the events of the storm.

Her gut instinct told her something was not right.

"How had it come to be the mizzenmast caught aflame so quickly?" she asked in concern. "Surely, your hands were well trained, so why had it not been put out before going up completely in flames?"

She saw his eyes narrow as he assessed what she had just asked him. She opened her mouth to apologize, but he spoke first.

"You're right, of course," he acknowledged, a gleam of respect in his eyes at her quick assessment of the situation. "There had been no noticeable lightning strikes near the ship. They had all occurred about a league off in the distance. Yet the officer in charge informed me that one of the crew had reported sighting strikes close by shortly before the mizzen caught fire. Everyone had been so occupied with saving the ship that no one noticed when the captain's servant fell overboard."

A tinge of regret entered his voice. "A rescue might have been attempted. Stafford was known to be one of the few hands who knew how to swim."

To himself, he wondered why no one had seen him. He could have been rescued. If only someone had noticed.

More disturbing to his thoughts were the unanswered questions about the steward's actions. Why had the servant not gone below deck as ordered and manned the bilge pumps? And was it truly a coincidence that the steward was washed away into the sea at the same time the mizzen caught fire?

These two disturbing events left him with an uneasy feeling. Someone aboard The Brunswick, he sensed, was not telling the truth . . . but why?

He swiftly concluded his narrative. "It was discovered Stafford was missing when he did not appear at morning mess. One of the noncommissioned crew replaced him at the captain's table. Do not ask me who it was. I cannot now recall."

"Captain Jackson has he, uh . . ." She hesitated, wondering how she was going to put forth this next question.

It was a private matter. One a lady was not supposed to speak about with a gentleman. But she had no choice. She had to ask.

For sure now, she thought gathering her courage, how true was the saying, which said that there are three diseases without shame—love, itch, and thirst. The one she wanted to ask about was none of these. For where did lust belong on the list?

Boldly, she decided to plunge ahead with her questioning. If it offended the gentleman, so be it. She needed to know. She could not be timid about seeking out the cause of the illness. If she waited any longer, he might take a sudden turn for the worse.

"Has Captain Jackson suffered recently from any sexual contagion? Has he been treating himself for any syphilitic complaints?"

The lieutenant looked up, startled by the question.

She met his gaze with a steady one of her own. She did not flinch. This was not some blithe question she asked. She needed to know.

As a wise woman, she had never been cloistered from learning about sexual contagions. She was familiar with the ways in which sailors slacked their penned up desires. She had at one time or another tried to treat them, often to no avail.

His dark eyebrows lifted briefly. He was surprised.

Quickly, he recovered. Nodding, he thought it over. He understood why she asked such an intimate question. It might indeed explain why Captain Jackson was in this sickly state. It was well-known that dangerous substances were recommended by naval surgeons and wise women to cure illnesses and ease pain.

Poisonous night shades, arsenic, belladonna and opium were some of the deadly plants recommended for such use. The toxins were at times effective in fighting sexual contagions. But they had to be used carefully. Improperly taken and they could quickly kill the patient.

"Nay, not to my knowledge," he answered honestly. "He is a man dedicated to the sea. He's had these past few months little time for female companionship. The captain knows his duty to the Admiralty, his ship, and to those serving beneath him. He's never been one to idly fritter away his time with loose women."

What he did not add was that Captain Jackson kept a mistress. Her name was Fiona Foxworthy, a pert, young theatrical performer barely out of her teens. She lived in a townhouse Captain Jackson rented in Portsmouth. She was the only woman in the commander's life.

Those who did know the light-skirt in question did not ask if she had other lovers. It was well known that the talented Fiona happily amused herself with several men. These gentlemen were her security. They stood in the captain's shadow. They were ready to take his place lest he should unexpectedly pass away at sea. That was a likelihood that could occur to any seaman, no matter how experienced. And Fiona, the daughter of a naval gunner, knew it better than most.

When Robert asked how he felt about the dancer's

fickle ways, the older officer shrugged off his young mistress's other admirers with an insightful remark.

"Fiona needs other men to amuse her. Aye, she's a vain little puss. I cannot reprimand her. 'Tis her way of keeping herself happy whilst I am away . . . I'll not deny her the small group of admirers she has. Aye, when I am back on land, 'tis only then I demand she become mine alone."

Robert put thoughts of Captain Jackson's young mistress aside. She couldn't be the cause of the illness. It wasn't possible. He turned his attention back to the wise woman.

"It has been more than six months since our last visit to Portsmouth. Thus most unlikely Captain Jackson caught any contagion of that kind," he explained. "He simply has not had an opportunity to be intimate with any woman. We've been out on the open sea these past several months as part of a blockade run. When we did take leave, he showed no interest in visiting the harbor trollops."

"I see," she said thoughtfully.

She ceased her questioning about Captain Jackson's love life. Whatever had brought about the present illness must have happened aboard The Brunswick.

"Is he well liked by the crew?" She glanced down at the ill officer who now slept fitfully by the hearth.

It was difficult to imagine anyone wanting to harm their commanding officer. Unless someone had an evil grudge against him, there would be no reason to wish him ill. Sailors usually respected their commanders. They were like demi-gods on the high seas.

"As much as any man in his position . . . he's a superb navigator. Controlled when under fire, a fair judge, he treats the men better than most captains. He is by all accounts a most excellent commanding officer to work under."

"'Tis good to hear," she said, shaking her head remorsefully.

"Why? Is he going to die?"

"Nay, I think not . . . but someone does want your commander dead."

"What! What do you mean?" he asked, shocked at her comment.

She tried to calm him. Her mother was resting in the other room. She was recovering from lung fever. The last thing she wanted was to disturb her.

"For sure now, there is no way of my putting it more delicately. But I must tell you although it may be painful to hear . . . someone is trying to kill him. This villain may very well have started after your last victory."

"Are you certain?"

She nodded in affirmation. Unable to look him directly in the eye, she fingered her woolen skirt.

"It was undoubtedly done by one of the ship's hands. Only someone aboard could have done this shameful act. It could not have been done any other way. One of The Brunswick's hands is a villain, sir," she said calmly.

"And this person has taken the opportunity and added poison to Captain Jackson's food. I could not believe it at first myself, until I looked at his tongue. Even then I had to consult with my mother to be sure. The swollen tongue, the stomach cramps, the loss of sensation in the limps, as well as the fact that no one but himself is ill. Aye, they are all signs pointing to one disturbing truth . . . your captain is slowly being poisoned to death, Lieutenant."

She glanced over at the slumbering man. He looked fragile and pale in the glow of the hearth fire. Sadly, she shook her head.

Why would anyone wish to do him harm? she wondered. What had brought about this hateful act?

Who could want to purposefully hurt the commander?

"Any other gentleman with less than the strong constitution your captain here enjoys . . ." She left the rest unsaid, shrugging her slender shoulders.

What more could she add? It was evident what would have happened.

"He would have been dead by now," he concluded. A burning anger raged inside his calm exterior. One of The Brunswick's crew had done this. It was an act of mutiny.

He bit out, "What you're saying is this was no random act. It was selective, meant to bring about his sudden demise."

She silently nodded in agreement.

He fisted his hands in pent-up frustration, ready to fight. His mouth was set in a firm line of grim determination. He had a duty to Captain Jackson. At that moment he silently vowed to discover who'd poisoned one of the most able commanders and strategists in his majesty's service. He would personally see to it that the assassin was drawn, quartered, and finally hanged from the highest yardarm for his crime.

"No one treats a commanding officer in his Majesty's Royal Navy this way," he declared. "And no one lays a finger against my commander without receiving retribution. Not while I live and breathe! This treasonous act will not go unpunished. I will ferret out the villainous snake and make him pay dearly for his treachery!"

Chapter 2

Sarah sat down beside the commander, clasping and unclasping her hands. She looked over at the deathly ill sea captain. This healing was going to be more difficult than lancing a boil. All her expertise and skill with the sick and dying was about to be put to practice on the captain. She seldom gave much hope for the recovery of such a gravely ill man.

Aye, it's going to take a miracle. And will this English officer trust me enough to let me try and heal his commander?

"He's very ill, Lieutenant Smythe," she said plainly. "I'm going to need your help if we are to save his life. He is in very grave danger."

"I'll do anything you ask, if you think you can save him."

"Good." She nodded approvingly. "Some of the requests I may ask of you will—well, they'll be a wee bit unconventional for an Englishman."

She looked him over carefully, trying to discern his thoughts about what she'd just said. He didn't respond. His face remained emotionless, indecipherable.

"They may, however, save your commander's life," she added.

"Then I will follow your instructions to the letter, ma'am."

He bowed in respect.

"Unquestioningly, Lieutenant?" she prodded. She wanted to make certain he would help her. She didn't need some high-handed English officer getting in her way.

Even if he does have, she had to silently admit to herself, *a form that the legendary Irish giant Finn Mac Cool himself would have appreciated.* Aye, the first mate standing before her was easy on the eye, with well-defined muscles and manly grace. He had an undercurrent of focused energy. It silently bespoke of his ease in giving commands and having them obeyed without question. He was clearly a very dangerous man. This was not someone who would tolerate being crossed.

She had to be cautious. For who knew what harm he might choose to do if his captain should suddenly die? Perhaps he would take all his frustrations out on her?

Warily, she eyed the muscles bulging up from his arms—aye, the outward form of a man never revealed the heart inside. He may be pleasing to the eye, but what of his character?

"I will do whatever you ask," he said, as if reading her thoughts.

His tone of voice told her he would not accept any refusal on her part. He was determined. She would be the one to heal his comrade.

"As if they were orders given directly by him . . ." With a nod, he indicated the sleeping form of his superior officer.

"Then let us begin . . . I will have to leave ye and go to the *teach an alais.*"

He gave her a puzzled look.

She smiled and explained, "It is the sweat hut where we'll try to remove the poison harming your captain. But first, I must fetch water and peat. We'll take him when the gale has abated. In an hour's time, it should be ready."

He nodded, not looking at her.

She could tell he did not fully comprehend the

enterprise they were about to undertake. She hoped he was a man of his word and would do what she asked. This was going to be complicated. The patient was already in a fragile state.

Aye, this English officer has no choice but to obey me—that is if he truly wishes to save his commander's life.

* * *

The harsh rain had diminished to a hazy mist. Cold mud seeped unpleasantly up through her wooden clogs. The wind had eased enough to let her walk unimpeded to the well. There she drew fresh water into a bucket.

She carried it into a small beehive-shaped stone building. It was built from island rock as the cottage was. The sweat hut was about seven feet high in a circular corbel shape with a small chimney hole in the top of the stone-slated roof.

She lit a fire in the center using dried peat. It would take a few hours to heat the hut sufficiently for its purpose. It would be used to sweat the poison out of the ailing seaman.

These stone huts were called *cathair* or *caiseal*. They'd been built by the corbelling process. It required placing one stone on top of another, bringing them closer and closer to one another as they were stacked. The huts were finished when they were finally roofed with long slabs of stone, filling in the remaining gaps on the curved top.

Spaces had been purposefully left between the stones for air ventilation. The hut was heated by the open turf fire located in the middle. No mortar or mud swaddle was used. The stones were placed in an outward manner to cause the rain to smoothly run down the structure. Despite its small size, it was a solid dwelling.

Three hours later, she gently woke the first mate. He was dozing by the hearth fire by his captain's side. His

Beverly Adam

dark head lay against his arm. She suspected that he was used to grabbing sleep whenever he could.

She shook his shoulder.

He sleepily opened his eyes, re-orienting himself to his surroundings. The wise woman stood next to him. The peat fire in the hearth, he noted, was now a pile of low burning embers.

"'Tis time," she said. "You must undress yourself and Captain Jackson. Clothe him in this nightshirt. The hut will be very hot, much like a steaming lobster pot. You need not be afraid of catching lung fever."

She went ahead of him and removed the burnt out peat from the sweat hut with a small shovel. She laid down sweet smelling dried rushes and placed them on the dirt floor to protect their feet. Refilling the bucket of water, she placed it by the open fire. All was now ready for the ailing sea captain.

Dressed only in his white naval breeches, Lieutenant Smythe hoisted Captain Jackson up to a standing position. He half-carried the ill man to the sweat hut. The captain had lost a great deal of weight since his sickness began.

The entryway to the building was small and tight. Robert had to crawl in on his hands and knees to enter. Muscles straining, he pulled the captain in after him.

It was tight and cramped inside. This was the first time he'd been in one of the caiseal. He eyed the walls in admiration at the symmetrical way the stones closely fit together. Carefully, he sat Captain Jackson on a low wood bench.

Sarah joined them. She wore a thin cotton camisole. A black wool shawl known as a comfy was wrapped protectively about her. She took the long garment off and seated herself.

He was about to question her attire, she could tell, but tactfully refrained.

[30]

The lieutenant kept to his promise not to question her peculiar decisions. She could not look at him directly in the eye. She lowered her eyelashes demurely, aware of his half-unclad state.

The intimacy of the situation was not one she was used to. Usually, she treated elderly patients, sick children, ailing mothers, and the occasional diseased seaman. Having a handsome, half-clad English officer seated next to her was not customary.

She'd been brought up in a household comprising only of women. She was keenly aware of his masculine presence. He was different, foreign to her senses. Like a male version of a siren, he was beautiful and completely enticing.

Although she was considered to be a bit of a flirt back in her home village, enjoying exchanges of friendly banter with the opposite sex, she nonetheless respected polite society's strict conventions. She never did anything that would set the gossipmongers' tongues clacking. She respected herself and her work as a wise woman too much to risk any negative talk.

Experience taught her that the villagers were suspicious of her, an outsider. She had to be above reproach around her patients' watchful families. She never gave them any reason to doubt her motives, but she was also dedicated to saving lives and sometimes that meant overcoming any feelings of modesty on her part. She knew that allowing Lieutenant Smythe to see her barely clad figure in the thin cotton chemise was unusual and brazen. But she quickly shrugged off any thoughts of wrongdoing. *This is not the time to be timidly prudish or troubled by the conventional rules of polite society.* Hadn't he asked for her help? Now she was going to provide it.

She was seated in this cramped hut, sweating with a patient on the brink of death. The good Lord help her, he had best get used to the idea of her breaking a few rules. They were not worth a half-shilling of good to his captain in here.

She glanced over at the first mate.

His body glistened from the rain and his own perspiration, dripping off his well-shaped chest. The first officer's skin shone from the steam. His skin was the color of polished bronze in the light of the hut's fire. Aye, he was too handsome by far . . .

Inwardly, she sighed. *Heaven help me . . . he is built like a veritable god, a young Adonis come to life.* For sure, Lieutenant Smythe had a powerful presence. One she was not accustomed to being around in a long time.

Three months ago she'd left her village when her mother was struck down by lung fever and returned home to care for her. Of late the young wise woman's life had resembled that of a recluse. She had completely devoted herself to healing. She'd been cut-off from the rest of the healthy living world. The sight of the half-clad lieutenant was like seeing land after being a long time at sea. He was a refreshing and attractive presence.

Diverting herself from the sight of the half-clad officer, she rose to close up the small entrance with a few layers of sod bricks. The rain was drizzling lightly. Water splattered into small puddles outside the hut.

Returning, she checked on Captain Jackson's condition. He appeared to be in a stable state. The deliriums had passed. Fervently, she hoped the sweating would rid him of the poison before any damage was done to his vital organs.

She forced herself not to be distracted by the handsome man next to her.

If you are not careful, you'll end up making a complete cake of yourself. He's given no indication he has noticed you, other than when he first laid eyes on you—nay, he would swim for his ship if he thought you had any interest in him as an unattached gentleman. An Irish wise woman does not have a wee bit of hope of attracting such a man. Aye, even if he is like whiskey for the eyes.

Secretly, although she would rather feed him her favorite goat than admit it, she wanted him to look at her. She wanted him to meet her steady gaze with one of his own. She could not help but wonder what would happen if he should do so.

At last he broke the silence between them.

"Tell me, how old is this sweat hut? Did you fashion it yourself or was it built by one of your ancestors?" he asked.

He was familiar with the old stone dwellings. The rocky green land of the southern coast contained the scattered relics of Ireland's ancient past. Circle ruins, stone beehive-shaped huts, and sea-weathered stone pillars, whose original purposes were long forgotten, had become part of local legends and superstitions.

Many of the ruins dotting the verdant hills were now used as animal holding pens. Some of the sacred places, once built by early Celtic pagans, evangelizing Christians had turned into respected churches and monasteries. As for the smaller, less well-built huts and burial mounds, they were believed to be the cursed homes of the wee fairy folk, the *daoine sidhe*.

He was, while trying to find a neutral subject of conversation, genuinely interested. He knew that there weren't many who looked kindly upon the ruins. The locals at the harbor tavern had warned him away from visiting them.

The wariness they felt towards the stone structures was evident in their eyes. They believed fairies and other magical creatures still practiced mischief upon unsuspecting mortals. The round stone *raths* were carefully avoided and due to superstitions, left undisturbed.

"I would not be going there if I were you, Commander," declared a local fisherman in an ominous tone. "The wee ones haunt them, sir. It's their fairy fort."

"To be sure, even if ye were to pay me a whole pile o' silver, I wouldn't go near their rath," warned the local bartender, passing him a dram of ale.

"Aye, stay away from them, Lieutenant," cautioned another of the older fishermen standing next to him at the tavern bar. "They might put ye under a powerful *gessa,* one of their dreaded curses. They've been known to bewitch men down to their cavern homes below to dance with their master, the Devil. Aye, stay clear o' the fairy rings, Lieutenant. There be terrible ancient magic about there."

Now he was sitting inside one of those dangerous huts. He could not help but wonder if perhaps he too was about to be cursed. Was he about to fall under a magic spell? Or suffer an even more interesting fate? Perhaps become enchanted by the charming Irish woman seated next to him?

He looked over at Sarah. The wise woman's hair gleamed gold in the pale light. Her fair skin was smooth like a well-polished stone. Aye, he thought, it would not be difficult to fall under any spell she might cast upon him. It would, he had to admit, undoubtedly be a pleasure.

"No Celt built this hut," she said, answering his question about its original builders. "It was created by invading Norse men hundreds of years ago. They once lived here on Varrik Isle. They used it to plunder local coastal villages and monasteries. The Norse realized this was a secure lookout post. In due time, we, and other healing folk, came here to use it to help with such maladies as the stiffening of the joints, which my mother and other elders suffer from."

A self-deprecating smile appeared at the corners of her mouth.

"Unlike you Norman English, we Irish have never been very large in size. In ancient times, they say, a man was only a few hands tall—aye, this hut suits our small Celt statures. It's good to cleanse one's body of impurities by sweating."

He changed the subject, thinking of the other lady she had spoken with.

"Tell me of the lady who lies in the cottage. You say she's your mother?"

"Aye, that she be . . . she is the renowned healer, Gladys Clogheen of Varrik-on-Suir."

"Then how is it that you know so much about healing?" he asked, astonished.

"As I told you, sir, I'm Gladys's adopted daughter, Sarah Duncan. I was named after the fisherman who found me, but 'twas herself, my adopted mother, who christened me with the name, Sarah. When no one laid claim to me, she took me in as her own. In time, I trained as her apprentice," she amended with a small smile. "The villagers with whom I live with on the mainland say 'tis because I'm a changeling fairy."

"A changeling?"

She nodded. "I was found adrift in a wee tar boat like Moses in the bulrushes. Duncan, my godfather, brought me to my mother right after I was found. No one else knew what to do with me—I cried all the time. They say the minute he laid me in my mother, Gladys's, arms I stopped."

"Indeed," he said, raising his eyebrows at this queer remark.

"Aye, I suppose you would find it to be so . . . the villagers have crafted their own fanciful tale as to the

facts. They believe the fey left me adrift in order to steal
healing knowledge away from a wise mortal, my mother.
They say that I'll return one day to my cavern home
beneath the earth and bring it back to the daione sidhe,
the wee hidden folk. Then I'll reign there as their queen,
cleverly bewitching mortal men and women folk."

"Are you telling me you're a . . . a fairy?" he asked,
incredulous. "And your mother, a renowned healer, is
um . . . a witch?"

"Aye, so I've been told. Although, because I've
been left in this mortal shape for so long, it is rather
doubtful I shall ever return to my fairy home," she
replied, a merry twinkle in her bright, blue eyes.

She looked directly at the English officer before her,
unashamed of her rather dubious parentage. She was
accustomed to it. It was a familiar part of her life.

The wise woman had nothing to hang her head
about. In truth, being an abandoned orphan was
something not worth fretting over. She knew who she
was. The name the villagers called her by—Wise Sarah,
said it all. She was the renowned healer, Gladys
Clogheen's adopted daughter and apprentice. What more
was there to know?

"Incredible . . . ," he said under his breath.

"Aye," she agreed.

Her mother, Gladys, had never tried to understand or
tolerate the superstitious fancies of the fearful villagers.
She looked equally down on them all. The famous
healer took herself far, far too seriously to mingle with
ordinary folk. She preferred to keep her own company,
never spending any time with those who led normal
lives.

In the end, sadly misunderstood, suspected of
cursing their livestock and blamed for a sundry of other
problems, the local people distrusted Gladys, except
when they needed her skills. And the healer wisely

sought out the more tranquil life of an island hermit.

She chose to live at a safe distance from others. She carefully picked the Island of Varrik, located a league off the western coast of Ireland. The remote spot proved to be exactly what her mother wanted. It proved a secure haven from meddlesome folk.

The tiny island was a refuge from those who might stupidly try to persecute the healer. Several times the superstitious had tried to have Gladys imprisoned for practicing witchcraft. Although she vehemently denied doing such heathen tomfoolery, they continued to persecute her.

During Sarah's childhood, angry mobs twice set their cottage on fire. Hooligans had also tried to force both of them to drink urine and other toxic brews. Time and again they'd been released because of overwhelming lack of evidence. No one could prove that either one of them was a witch, or in her case, a changeling fairy.

The imposing English mayor of the village set them free. Once he stood in the center of an angry mob, asserting his authority with a troop of armed redcoats.

He said, "I won't tolerate any more of this mumbo jumbo nonsense. Understand this once and for all. Anyone who touches these women will be clapped in irons and put immediately in prison!"

It was under this dire threat that she and her mother were at last left in peace.

From time to time those who believed her mother to be a wicked minion of the Devil appeared at their door. Superstitious villagers, who held evil in their hearts against their neighbors, persisted in troubling them.

Her mother muttered angrily at one of the darkly dressed *make-baits,* one of those witless fools who wanted her to cast a hex upon one of his neighbors in order to make him feel powerful. He was a long-nosed man who broke her usual night's slumber with his clamor for spiteful revenge.

"Now listen to me, you moonstruck bit of annoying jackanapes. I want ye to take your presumptuous arse off of my clean steps, and I'm warning ye to never come here and disturb my slumber again! Or I'll—"

"But I've brought some gilt, mistress," whined the man from under his black hood. He held up some money in the moonlight for her to see, "to pay for your fee of hexing that troublesome neighbor of mine whose dog took a bite out of me the other day."

He then produced a dead animal.

"I brought this rat to hang over his door to hex him with," he added in a dramatic voice. "So you can turn it into a rabbit and cast a dark spell over his herd of cattle. I did all this to please you, o' grand mistress of the night."

Visibly upset at these thoughts of malice, the wise woman uttered several angry oaths in Irish. It was well worth noting that her mother's incensed utterances were worthy of the forked tongue Devil with whom she was supposed to be associating.

"Now get off before I throw some magic dust upon your ridiculous puny hide!" she yelled out at him. "You're nothing but a poor wretch of a man. Aye, and I don't blame that dog for taking a bite out of you, neither. If I could, the good Lord above knows, I surely would like to myself!"

The make-bait tartly answered back that she was nothing but an ugly old hag who should be burned at the stake. And he would be the first one to light the fire and dance around it while she burned. Suddenly, he shut his mouth.

Bug-eyed, he stared at her, visibly gulping with fear.

The irritated wise woman raised one hand in the night air, making a menacing gesture towards the small sack she held in the other. She uttered something darkly in Irish. Her face was grim. The make-bait had disturbed her slumber and used vile language about her. Now he was going to pay for his misdoings.

The troublemaker took one look at her and the menacing sack she held. He quickly came to a decision. It was time to depart. Scurrying down the island hill, he ran to the beach.

Quickly, he pushed his small skiff out onto the smooth moonlit water. He looked fearfully behind him. What if the horrible witch took to cursing him? Aye, and use that magic powder she held aloft in her hand?

He put his hands protectively over his privates.

She could curse them right off.

Wiping his sweaty brow, he rowed quickly away. He was lucky to escape with his body and soul intact. He swore to himself that in the future, he would stay away from troublesome black magic.

When her mother reentered the cottage, Sarah peeked into the sack. She recognized the contents immediately and smiled. It contained nothing more than common itching powder made from plant fibers from the pods of a tree.

The wise woman had thought to use the prank to inflict irritation and doubt. With admiration, she had to admit her mother had used a clever trick against the superstitious nincompoop.

After learning all she could from her adopted mother, Sarah finally left the Island of Varrik. During her travels, she came upon Urlingford village in the rolling, green hills of Kilkarney, Ireland. She decided she could live comfortably in the small village and quickly forged alliances with both the influential priest of the parish, who baptized her in the church in front of the entire village.

Not much had changed in the small Irish village for hundreds of years, except instead of having Celtic chieftains ruling over them, it was now the puritanical

English. The powerful ruler of the seven seas forced reluctant Ireland in 1801, by the Act of Union, to become part of their empire building.

The English, afraid the Catholic aligned countries of Portugal and Spain, would try to take control of this kingdom to their north, imported Puritans from England and Scotland to colonize it. These in turn took iron-fisted control over the now impoverished Irish. As a result the native Irish Catholics lost most of their land and rights.

Despite local superstitions, the villagers liked and respected her. No one dared to harm a hair on her golden head. Secretly, they were proud of their wise woman. In time, she became as well known and respected as her mother.

To add to her status, she was under the protection of the wealthy spinster, Lady Beatrice O'Brien. The rich lady in turn was soon to be bride of the new Earl of Drennan and had a great deal of influence over the entire parish. The match between the new English lord and their local Irish gentlewoman was much anticipated. Many predicted it would be beneficial for the future of both the Catholic Irish, as well as the Protestants.

"You do not live here?" Robert asked.

She shook her head, steamed blonde ringlets framing her oval face. She brushed a loose tendril aside. "Faith, no. I rent a small cottage in Kilkarney. I came back here because my mother sent for me. She's been suffering from putrid lung fever and needed my help."

Sweat dripped down their faces from the steam. She reached for the dipper hanging from the side of the bucket of water. After taking a sip, she passed it to him.

He gave some to Captain Jackson. The water slid down the semiconscious officer's face.

"And where do you originally hale from, Lieutenant?"

"I'm currently in command of a fifth rate naval

frigate, The Brunswick. We're harbored in Dingle for a few days for repairs to our mizzenmast and hull. Once finished, we'll continue our journey south and sail down to Portsmouth, England, our journey's end. It is there I will take leave of my command and crew, handing her back over to the Royal Admiralty."

He shook his head in bitter disappointment.

"It is the first time we've been in friendly waters in over eight months. We've been battling the Spanish and French since we left England, as well as chasing American blockade runners out of our waters. We were to go ashore for a short leave, but then this happened," he said, gesturing to the ailing man at his side. "Several of my gunners recommended your mother, Gladys Clogheen, to me. She was my last hope to save Captain Jackson."

"Are you married? Do you have family waiting back in England?"

"Nay, I'm a bachelor. I suppose you could say I'm faithfully married to the sea, ma'am."

She smiled, strangely relieved at his unmarried state. She didn't want to think of a frowning wife back in England glowering at her as she took the liberty of glancing at his well-proportioned bare chest. The tanned face of the seasoned naval officer and his dark hair gave him the dangerous appearance of an unruly pirate, not a proper English officer.

The first lieutenant's masculine features had the intensity of one used to spending cold nights on watch. He had a deep crease above his brow, earned by long hours of looking out for enemy frigates, icebergs, and deadly, jagged rock formations. Small creases fanned out from his keen eyes, etched from squinting into the distance under the bright glare of the sun that glinted off the waters. She had the impression he was never fully at ease.

His handsome face was made all the more rugged by

his nose. It had a slight bump at the top of the brim. An act of violence had caused the imperfection. She later learned it had been broken during close hand-to-hand combat on a warship's quarter-deck. He'd been battling against marauding Portuguese pirates. It dominated the center of his face along with an intelligent high forehead. His sweeping black brows, arched over his deep brown eyes. Those same alert eyes, now observed her with searching intensity.

Nervously, she twisted a small gold ring on her right hand.

He noticed the small ring for the first time. It was a simple gold band featuring two hands holding up a crowned heart. The one the wise woman wore pointed towards the fingertips, a sign she was available to court.

If it had been turned the other way around, it would have indicated that she was spoken for. Her heart therefore closed, already claimed. Although this might have been the case once, apparently it was not now.

"Is your mother from Claddagh?" he asked, familiar with the ring's origins. They were heirlooms given as love tokens from that western part of Ireland near Galway.

She shook her head.

"I was once betrothed to a man who was," she sadly explained, remembering her dead fiancé. "John Maxwell was his name. And for a time he was a blacksmith in our village. A friend talked him into joining the service. He worked as an armorer aboard a third-rated warship. He died quite suddenly from typhus brought aboard by men pressed into service. I was sent word several months ago. It was about the same time when my mother fell ill."

She recalled how the dark news of her mother's illness had reached her at Brightwood Manor, her friend Lady Beatrice O'Brien's home. Bea' insisted on ordering a carriage to drive her south. She embraced her friend warmly when she left, not knowing when she would return to see her again. From there she hopped on a fishing boat to convey her to the island. Upon her arrival, news was delivered by her godfather concerning her fiancé's death.

Worried half-to-death over her mother, who'd been struck down with lung fever, and sick at heart over the loss of her fiancé, she'd been utterly alone. Gnawing fear and grief filled her days. It was one of the darkest times in her life.

"Having no daughters of her own, John's mother asked me to take the ring as a keepsake to remember him by—" she could not finish what she was about to say. It hurt too much.

She would have been married and perhaps already with child if he'd lived. He'd always been good to her. Despite being a large man with a rough and ready-to-fight exterior, John had had a tender heart underneath. Now he was gone and so too that promising future.

The ring's symbols in which the hands represented friendship, the crown, loyalty, and the heart, love, had lived up to its motto of 'let love and friendship reign supreme.' John had been good to her, protective and kind.

His mother had refused to take the ring back.

John's mother had said, closing her fingers around the ring, "Keep it, Sarah. He loved you so. It will be a good way to remember him by. I think you ought to know a charm was put upon the ring the day it was made. It's supposed to help the wearer find true happiness and love. I hope it will help ease some of your pain."

The grieving mother had smiled sadly, patting Sarah's hand. "One day ye'll wed and have a child of your own. When that day comes, write and let me know."

[43]

Out of respect to her deceased betrothed's mother, she continued to wear the ring. But she didn't believe any charm would help her find love again. There was no fairy-tale ending waiting for her. The ring only reminded her of how well she'd been cherished. In that manner, she'd been more blessed than most. Those who had suddenly lost loved ones at sea often had no such comforting knowledge.

"My condolences, ma'am," Robert said, breaking into her thoughts.

He knew many loyal men who had died. The war had taken its toll on the male population of the entire Union. No country had been spared.

He knew it was not action in battle that killed most sailors serving under the Union Jack. Deadly diseases, which quickly spread aboard the crowded quarters of the naval ships, did the greatest harm. They killed entire crews more effectively than any enemy cannon possibly could.

"Tell me of your family, Lieutenant Smythe," she said, not wishing to speak any further of her loss. "Are you from the titled gentry?"

"Nay," he answered with a dismissive shrug.

Titles meant nothing to him, except when backed by a superior officer's rank. Thankfully, the Royal Navy, unlike the army, did not permit the buying of commissions. To be made a superior officer, a seaman had to earn the title. Happily, there were very few pampered, silver spoon fed aristocrats to contend with on a naval vessel.

"The Smythe family tree is that of the middle branches of respectable society. It consists of mostly merchant seafarers. My father was master of his own ship and my uncle was a captain in the Royal Navy," he explained. "As to my mother's family, she was a master rope maker's daughter." He paused, thinking of the good-tempered lady who'd been his mother.

"My father doted on her. For what woman would cheerfully accept her husband being gone months at a time away at sea and bear him seven children without any thoughts of desertion? Not many, I'd wager."

His thoughts about the past darkened. "When my father was captured by the French and died in prison, I was almost a lad of twelve. My mother's brother took pity on us. He was a first lieutenant aboard a third-rated warship at the time and arranged for my older brother and myself to join the crew as midshipmen. So it was I who took to sea and the naval profession to earn my keep."

"Has it been a good trade?"

This was the first time she'd ever spoken at length with an English naval officer. Most of the other seamen she met from the Royal Navy were non-commissioned sailors in need of her help. Officers never spoke directly to her, especially the English ones.

Being an Irish woman meant she was far beneath their superior regard. She didn't even merit a courteous tip of the hat or a 'beg your pardon' when accidentally brushed up against on a crowded street. The English, everyone agreed, were an imperiously rude lot.

"The navy has been the very best of occupations," he answered proudly. "I've only had a few regrets concerning my choice. Aye, a man is never bored traveling the open seas. There are always new challenges to overcome, adventures aplenty to be caught up in. Although I must admit there have been times I'd have liked to have had someone to share my life with . . ."

He stopped his confession, astonished that he'd almost told her the pangs of loneliness he sometimes felt upon witnessing the happy reunions of other officers with their loved ones. Those poignant moments of returning home were when he almost wished he'd spent more time ashore to find himself a wife.

"You're a son of Neptune, Smythe. Your life belongs to the sea," interrupted Captain Jackson, barely croaking out the words.

He was fully conscious now, having revived in the sweat hut. The poison slowly loosened some of its deathly grip on him. He leaned weakly against his first mate, a smile on his cracked lips. He nodded his graying head in Robert's direction.

"This man has served under me as my first mate for the last two years, ma'am. He is one of the finest officers in his majesty's navy. And now I consider him to be my most loyal and true friend."

Droplets of sweat poured down his face. Looking over at the comely woman seated next to him, his light blue eyes shone with an appreciative manly twinkle.

"Don't be bashful, lad—come now, introduce me properly to the lovely lady," the ill officer said. "I find her company to be most agreeable."

The first mate nodded and smiled. He could well understand why the older seaman would be eager to meet the half-clad lady. Despite the sweat and dampness, the wise woman looked alluringly beautiful.

"Captain Jackson, I have the pleasure of presenting to you Mistress Sarah Duncan, adopted daughter of Gladys Clogheen of Varrik-on-Suir, one of Ireland's most renowned healers. She has just rescued you from an untimely demise."

The ill officer saluted her with trembling fingers, touching his sweating forehead.

"Sink me then, are you a bewitching temptress or an angel fallen from the heavens above, ma'am, for coaxing my poor body back to life?" the captain asked in a hoarse, yet merry voice. "For 'tis certain that without your help, I would have been launched into my watery grave by now."

"I am neither, sir. I'm simply a wise enough woman to have taken heaven's part in the matter and tried to secure your life solidly to earth as God so intended," she answered back unabashedly, passing a dipper of water to him.

His hand shook as he took it.

Water trickled down his chin as he lifted it to his mouth. He smiled at her. "Aye, 'tis a pleasure, ma'am, to make your acquaintance. I would stand, but in my present condition, I think it best I salute you from here on this solid bench. Lest I be mistaken, my two bandy legs have lost their strength."

"There is no need for you to make so grand a gesture, Captain Jackson. You are excused, sir. I am certain we will become better acquainted in due time while you recuperate here on my mother's island."

She stood and wrapped the long comfy shawl about her, preparing to depart the hut. The storm had diminished to a light breeze, the gale having abated.

"You will excuse me, gentlemen. I'll go now to prepare us some tea. It will help with the cleansing of the impurities attacking Captain Jackson's spleen."

Directing her attention to Robert, she added one final parting instruction, "Captain Jackson should remain just a little longer, Lieutenant. At the cottage, I will massage him with a special ointment. Drink plenty of water, Captain Jackson. It will help with your recovery."

Nodding a pleasant goodbye, she exited, leaving Robert to explain how they'd come to be in Ireland and on this small island.

Chapter 3

Upon her return to the cottage, Sarah was surprised to see her mother up and about, tidying the small main room with a reed broom. Gladys was dressed in a red wool skirt, dyed from the juice of elderberries and worn with a loose knitted tunic.

"Mother," she said, hurrying to her side, "are you certain you're well enough to be up in your condition and working?"

"I think I am, daughter," replied the wise woman, putting a copper kettle over the open hearth fire. "'Tis certain that I'll not lie comfortable while you deal with those English officers on your own. Nay, 'tis high time I was up and about. A bit of work will not do me any harm. I can feel my lungs becoming pure again. They no longer trouble me as much as they did, though I gasp like a fish on dry land. Aye, you did a splendid job of helping me come back to my former self. 'Tis proud I am of your healing skills."

"High praise indeed from the one who taught me," she said, giving her mother a warm, affectionate hug. She noted the expression on her mother's face change from that of soft tenderness to concern.

"What's the matter? It cannot be the strangers. The English captain appears to be warding off the shadow of death on his own and grabbing hold to life. As for the lieutenant, he's behaved like a proper gentleman, causing us no worries, but your face shows a lack of peace over something. What is it?"

"Aye, you've the right of it. It's this sorry business of Captain Jackson being poisoned, which is troubling me," confessed Gladys, looking her daughter over, feeling a pang of concern for their guests.

"I think the lieutenant will have his hands full. And not just with that poor sick man he brought here, but with the more dangerous concern of who did this to him. If I mistake not the determined gleam in his eyes, I would say that as soon as Captain Jackson is well enough, he'll be off trying to discover who did this evil deed."

"And that concerns ye?"

"Aye." Gladys nodded. "It was an evil person who dared to poison the captain of a royal naval frigate on his own vessel. He would have to be someone quite devious and villainously reckless to do so."

"Do you think that we might be of help to Lieutenant Smythe?"

Her mother looked her directly in the eye.

"Aye." She nodded solemnly. "When the time comes, you must go with them, Sarah. You're young and more capable than I. They need someone to tell them from whence the poison originally came. You could be the one to discover the evil person who did this to Captain Jackson."

"Me?"

"For sure, you would know what to look for. That is if it should be tried again. The taste, the texture, the smell of it when mixed in food and strong drink. 'Tis certain the lieutenant is a fine seafaring man, but he does not know how to discern poison in food. However, you do."

Gladys gave her daughter a significant look and slowly shook her head.

"Musha, musha, this troubles me to no end . . . the assassin may try again. If he should learn his failure is due to us, he might very well come looking for revenge.

Then we'll be caught good and tight in a noose of our own making, won't we?"

"Why?"

"We're vulnerable. Out here, alone, I can only protect myself but a little. As for you, even in that friendly village of yours, they can't protect you from the evil plans of a murderous madman."

The older wise woman looked darkly at her. Her face reflected her unease.

"Once it is known Captain Jackson didn't die and why he's still alive, we'll need to be more protective of our own lives. The assassin will assuredly be after us for foiling his plans. He'll be fearful and angry because of his failure."

"She's right, Mistress Duncan," Robert said as he helped Captain Jackson inside. "You and your mother will become the next targets on this villain's list. Once word gets out that you saved the commander's life, you'll have to be cautious. You won't know whom to trust."

"They must both come with us," said Captain Jackson in agreement.

"I have given it some thought and I have a better plan, Commander," replied the first mate. "You and Mistress Gladys will remain here. Thus enabling you to fully recover, purging the poison that has laid siege to you. Then when you've regained your full vigor, you'll join us in Portsmouth. In the meanwhile, I'll bandy about the lamentable news of your untimely death and try to uncover the evildoer."

"Are you mad?" protested Captain Jackson, alarmed.

He tried to stand up, but failed.

There was no strength in his legs. The limbs and muscles had been inactive for too long. "The Admiralty must be told the truth about my condition, Smythe. I cannot just up and disappear. This villain must be found!"

"*Demme*, Captain, I do not know who did this to you. It may very well be one of our own men," the first mate said gravely, his face taut with the earnest desire to sniff out the traitor. "He must be exposed and brought to justice before he does any further harm. Who knows who he may try to eliminate next?"

"You're in no state to take command of any ship, Captain," said Gladys firmly, seconding Robert's suggestion. The experienced wise woman contemplated the ill sea captain knowingly, assessing the state of his weakened body.

"You'd be putting yourself and your crew in grave danger if ye tried."

"What do you know of the matter, ma'am?" asked the offended officer, huffily. He coolly looked at the healer with all the frigid contempt his superior station granted him.

She obviously did not fully comprehend the complexity of the situation. She couldn't possibly grasp the importance. He had to get back to his command. His men needed him. He had to return to The Brunswick.

"My mother understands a great deal, sir," said Sarah, as if she could read his thoughts. "It was through her advice and training that I was able to save your life. I heartily agree with her and Lieutenant Smythe. Ye would do better to remain here, sir, continuing your cleansing. We Irish have a saying, ''Tis better to have fifty enemies outside the house than one hiding within.' And you have one aboard your ship with a nasty habit of trying to kill you, Captain."

She frowned and added, "Lieutenant Smythe cannot be expected to protect you, run a warship, and chase down an assassin all in the same breath. For who knows if the next time this devil won't succeed? And then where will the blessed Admiralty be minus one of its valuable naval captains?"

Giving the sick officer time to think over what they said, she quietly passed him a fired clay cup containing the hot sage brew she had prepared.

She poured one for herself and the others. They all sat in glum silence. She drank her tea. It tasted slightly bitter with a lingering smoky peat flavor from the hearth's turf fire.

"'Tis good," said Captain Jackson in a conciliatory manner. He owed these women his life. He checked his temper and frustration.

Being a man of strategy, he quietly considered his options. He was gravely ill and as weak as a new born lamb. That fact settled poorly on his manly pride. He wanted action.

"Sage has been used for hundreds of years for healing, Captain Jackson. It was often said, 'How can a man die who grows sage in his garden?'" commented Gladys, bringing him tactfully back into the conversation. "In due time, you'll regain your full strength and resume your command. Then your time here will be but a brief, unpleasant memory."

"That is if the Admiralty hasn't taken me off the lists," said the officer with a tinge of bitterness. "If it had been any other man but Smythe here—well I'd have called him out as a mutinous traitor and his action of taking command a hanging offense. But as he has just saved my life, the noose, it would appear is around my neck."

He looked over at the young officer and shook his head. He had come to his senses. If Smythe had truly wanted to get rid of him, he could have simply left his sorry body aboard The Brunswick to slowly worsen and eventually die. Nay, he could not put the blame on his stalwart first mate.

"There are other posts, Captain Jackson. But there are no other commanders like you, sir. The Admiralty will want you back once you're again in full charge of your health," said Robert, knowing the full value of seasoned leadership and experience.

The ships and lucrative cargo Captain Jackson had managed to capture from the enemies of the United Kingdom made the commander of The Brunswick much respected by his fellow officers. Any man of his reputation was not readily put aside. He had influential friends in power. They would see to it he was not easily dismissed.

"You need not fear. Quick, able-minded captains who can provide the victories at sea that you've handed the navy are highly valued," he commented.

"Aye." Captain Jackson nodded slowly, seeing reason. "I suppose, 'tis true . . . but how I long to get my hands upon the villain who did this to me! I'd like to string him up from the highest topsail for all to see and let him die a lingering death."

"I give you my word, this would-be assassin will be brought to justice," said his first mate in earnest. "He'll be made to pay for his crime against you. Have no fear, sir. It will be taken care of before you once again walk on a quarter-deck. Of this, I promise."

Captain Jackson patted him on the shoulder.

He was reconciled, putting his personal frustrations aside. "Aye, I suppose you're right, Smythe. I will put my faith in you and in these ladies."

The conversation continued into the night concerning Captain Jackson's ideas as to when and how he may have been poisoned. Sarah carefully took notes of the conversation with an ink quill. She made a list of the people with whom he'd spent the last fortnight, the inns he'd patronized, the food and drink he had partaken of. She wrote down all that he could muster from memory concerning the days leading up to his illness.

It's going to be a bit like looking for a needle in a

haystack, she thought with a small weary sigh, looking over the notes when they finished. The sooner they began the search, the better. Captain Jackson and Gladys depended upon them unmasking this villain. She and the lieutenant must not fail. Far too much was at stake. *Muineann ga seift. Need teaches a plan.* Eventually, the lieutenant and she would have one.

She closed the notebook. She added it to the small stack of belongings she would take with her on the morrow. Once again she was ready to leave the safety of her childhood home.

*   *   *

The sun at last broke through bathing the island in its warming light. Sarah and her mother stood by the door of the cottage, her small traveling trunk sat at her feet. She said one final farewell to her mother, holding her close—hoping that the next time she saw her, it would be under happy circumstances with this danger behind them.

"Are ye certain that you'll be able to handle him?" she asked her mother, glancing worriedly over at Captain Jackson who sat by the hearth.

"Have no fear," her mother said, patting her reassuringly on the shoulder. "After a time we'll be like two old slippers sitting next to each other cozily by a fire. We'll warm up to each other and come to a mutual understanding. He may be cantankerous and proud, but as ye know, I've dealt with worse. Aye, I'll manage him fine."

"Aye, that you'll do," Sarah agreed with an affectionate smile.

It was true her mother had dealt with more difficult men than Captain Jackson. She trusted her mother's abilities to cope with the proud officer. How the two would manage was in her mother's capable hands.

Robert joined them. He picked up her small trunk, lifting it up onto his shoulder. He'd already said his farewells to the commander.

"Time we departed, Mistress Duncan. I want us gone before the next tide."

Kissing her mother on the cheek, she bid her one final goodbye.

Once more she was leaving her family home for an uncertain future. Knowing the explosive situation aboard The Brunswick, she wondered what dangers lay ahead for her.

She glanced over at the handsome profile of the young English officer. Disturbing doubts ran through her mind. They almost caused her to turn tail.

Could this determined English naval officer be trusted to take care of her? What problems would she be facing in helping him find the one who poisoned Captain Jackson? And would she later come to regret her decision to go with him?

From here on she would have to rely upon him for food, shelter, and companionship. If in any manner he should fail her—it would be devastating. She was going to have to count on him for both her comfort and safety. It depended entirely upon him as to how she was going to be treated by the ship's crew.

She chewed on her lower lip. *Indeed, I have cause to wonder if I mightn't be walking into a lion's den full of trouble.*

But the lieutenant's behavior towards her had been correct, entirely without fault, she reminded herself. Hopefully, he would continue to behave in a manner worthy of a gentleman when they were on board his ship, and he had promised her mother this morning he would take good care of her. Plus, if anything should happen to her, she suspected, Captain Jackson would, upon leaving her mother's island, make full retribution on her behalf.

She glanced over at his handsome profile as they

walked down to the beach. *Nay, I have no reason to be concerned. He will stand by his promise to protect and take care of me. The only one I need to worry about is that villain I have to ferret out. He's the one I need to be wary of. Not this gentleman.*

They sailed to the mainland in a pucan, a fishing boat built of oak. Sturdy and quick, it was about twenty-two feet in length. An experienced seaman, Robert had no difficulty maneuvering the small craft. The skies above them had cleared to a cloudless dark blue and a light breeze aided the sail.

Brought up on a tiny dot of an island, Sarah ably aided him by manning the rudder. In no time they were smoothly sailing into Dingle Harbor. Their voyage was a pleasant one until they started discussing the best way to introduce her to the crew.

At first she'd shaken her head in disagreement over the idea. Her arms tightly folded.

"You cannot possibly believe your crew will accept me as such," she said, when he first proposed the manner in which to introduce her.

She enumerated her reasons. "I'm of uncertain origin, the lowliest of the low in Ireland. I don't have either the family connections or wealth to entice you into doing me the honor of asking for my hand. You know, they'll think you a right, blithering fool to do so, Lieutenant."

The steady gaze he directed at her told her he would not be changing his mind.

She tried to remain calm and not lose her temper. *Aye, though there is no bone in the tongue, it has frequently broken a head. If I'm not careful, it will surely be my own I'll be hurting today.*

"You're an English naval officer with a promising future in the Royal Admiralty," she said aloud, trying to reason with him. "You, deciding to marry me—why 'tis far too incredible to be believed! They will think you've gone stark raving mad to tie yourself to someone so far beneath you. It would be plain ludicrous and—"

"You will pose as my betrothed," he cut in, determination lacing his speech. "I cannot explain to the crew this sudden change of attitude towards having an unmarried lady aboard, unless she be mine own."

He eyed her up and down. For some reason, he was angry at her remark. He didn't want her to belittle herself. She was a brave woman and he admired her for her healing skills and her intelligence. The circumstances of her birth mattered not to him. But the reaction of his crew did. She was too pretty by far to come aboard as a spinster. Just sitting there in the bow of the ship, he was having a hard time keeping himself from reaching out and touching her. He had to keep himself in check and set an example for his men to follow. "The men will think me hypocritical, making up rules to suit myself if I do otherwise. At the present moment, I cannot afford to have any of them questioning my actions. As acting master and commander of The Brunswick, I must be above reproach in everything I say or do if I want to maintain order and avoid a mutiny."

"Ye mean to say, you've never had any female companionship during your last two years at sea?" she asked, amazed.

She peered up at him. She couldn't fathom it. He was far too attractive and virile to be alone. She could discern no sign of any present illness about him. Nor had he indicated he did not enjoy female companionship. Gazing at his handsome face, she thought that any lady, unless she had a couple of loose tiles in the upper story, would want to spend time alone in his company.

Perhaps he kept a mistress? For some reason this made her upset. Of course he wouldn't just engage in dalliances with light-skirts. No, he was the kind of man who, no doubt, would keep a lover in a comfortable cottage or rooms for his return to port.

But not all men were so disciplined. Having been around busy harbor ports her entire life, she knew seamen brought not just their wives and sweethearts aboard their vessels, but also mistresses and prostitutes. Frequently, unable to get shore leave because of the Royal Navy's legitimate fear of the noncommissioned and impressed crew swimming for land, sailors sent for the soiled doves to come to them aboard their overcrowded warships.

Desperate for female companionship, they paid the trollops of the port to visit them. Small enterprising vessels, known as "drab tail trulls" were loaded with friendly strumpets and made frequent calls upon the visiting vessels. A seaman simply had to scrounge together enough coin to pay for the services the women provided.

Firsthand she had witnessed the after effects of these thoughtless indulgences of the flesh. She'd tried to cure the sexual contagion that ravaged these short-lived liaisons. Often she was called upon in the last stages of the disease to provide laudanum to ease some of the painful suffering of the dying.

The end result of these relationships was a temporary reprieve from poverty and hunger for the women, many of whom were seamen's widows. Untimely deaths were common. She'd estimated that the career of a harbor strumpet walking the streets lasted no more than three years.

"My men may frequent such loose company, but I do not," he said bluntly. He did not look her directly in the eye. His statement made her smile inwardly. Clearly, his preference in ladies was not a subject he desired to discuss at length with her, but she was pleased that he was careful all the same.

"The practice of having ladies aboard is one I've been trying to persuade Captain Jackson to cease. They bring nothing but disruption aboard. The men grow careless when the fairer sex are around and catch diseases of the foulest kind. Not to mention they behave foolishly. I've lost count the number of times one of the hands has drunkenly climbed the topsails to impress a tittering female, only to fall off, and break one or more bones in his idiotic body."

There had been times he wished he could have prevented some of the more outstanding stupidities. "Ladies interfere with the running of the ship. They smuggle aboard strong spirits, get under foot, and in general make a ghastly nuisance of themselves. They're nothing but trouble."

In his younger midshipman days he'd been a bit reckless with his relationships. He'd met ladies of questionable virtue on his many voyages in different ports and island harbors throughout the British Empire. However, he'd quickly seen the foolishness of engaging with any of these light-skirts.

"But, sir," she interrupted, "if having a lady on board is such a bother, why must I pose as your betrothed? Why not simply pass me off as a friend of your family's or even a relative? Perhaps as someone who is visiting you for a brief time?"

At this remark he laughed derisively, a wolfish grin twisting his lips. A sparkle of manly humor appeared in his dark brown eyes. She was sitting demurely next to him, the sun lighting her hair from behind. He looked her over appraisingly. Pass herself off as a friend? Was she mad? When was the last time she looked at herself? She was a young woman and too comely by far for his men, let alone himself, to try and ignore.

The cool north wind had colored her pale cheeks to a becoming shade of pink. She was prettier than any portrait he'd ever viewed in a picture gallery. In his eyes she outshone those so-called beauties of the first circle, *le haute monde*, or high society.

The ladies who frequented the royal court and pleasure gardens were base and commonly coarse, in his opinion. The ladies of the upper echelon wore low décolletage and wetted gowns in fashionable salons in order to expose their voluptuous charms. By exhibiting themselves, they caused titters of scandalous delight among the English courtiers. They hoped to gain more notoriety and rich patrons in this manner. By comparison, this simply dressed Irish colleen in her homespun wool dress was one of the most naturally charming and desirable women he had ever encountered.

"As my friend," he repeated softly aloud, with a hint of amusement. "Nay, 'tis not possible, dear lady. No one for an instant would believe it! You're like a perfectly plump chicken, ready to be plucked and devoured."

His teeth gleamed in the sunlight, lips smiling upwards in good humor. The charming minx was trying to dissuade him!

The tone of his voice darkened at the mere thought of her coming aboard as an unmarried spinster. What she was suggesting was entirely unthinkable and too dangerous by far, and with a killer running loose on board the ship, who knew what perils she might face? No, he had to protect her at all costs.

"My fellow officers, let alone my crew, would slit my throat if they thought you were anything else but my fiancée. Aye, you need to be good and tied to me in their thoughts by the sacred vows of God. If you come aboard as unspoken for . . . well, that Mistress Duncan, would be preposterous. The suggestion will not be contemplated."

"I can handle myself, sir," she said bravely, straightening her back.

She thought of the switchblade she kept hidden. It was strapped to her right stocking. She kept it as a safety precaution. One she did not wish to tell him about. She had once been forced to put it to good use.

"The minute your feet touch the top deck, you will become my betrothed," he repeated in a voice that brooked no nonsense. It was said in such a stern manner, she was almost certain he made use of it on his crew. It was effective. It made her reconsider.

Silently, she mulled over the possibilities of defending herself against randy seamen. In close quarters it would be hard to do. If she were cornered by one of the men, where would she run? How would she protect herself if more than one became involved?

The frigate would be too small to avoid close contact with the hands. A large man could physically overcome her weapon and then what? She shivered, remembering that one time in Dublin when she had sliced the hand of a man who had attacked her from behind. Although she had managed to escape and run away, never again did she venture about without a paid escort. She also had to admit the lieutenant could not be expected to be always next to her. He had responsibilities, a crew and ship to command, as well as a villain to unmask. He could not be expected to play nursemaid and have her tied to him all day.

She shook her head, knowing the reality of the situation. No, she would have to take care of herself.

He put a hand beneath her chin.

She looked up into his eyes and met his even gaze.

"Please, don't disobey me in this, ma'am," he said. "I am now in command and it is you who must obey. Do you understand? I must be very firm about this before we board. This concerns your safety as well as my crew's."

He smiled, taking the edge off of his speech. "A beautiful lady can easily break half-a-dozen sailors' hearts merely by smiling at them. And your smile, I daresay, could cause an epidemic of fatalities."

He removed his hand.

"Will you do as I ask? And be kind to both me and my crew? So no blood will be spilled over you?"

"Aye, sir," she replied softly, losing herself for a moment.

He'd just called her "beautiful." She felt a delightful heat course through her entire body. And it was not the sun's brightness that had brought about this sudden warmth. It was the afterglow of his compliment.

Slowly, she nodded in reluctant agreement.

"I will do as you wish, Lieutenant Smythe. I'll pretend to be your betrothed."

"Good," he said, catching sight of the bow of a sleek modern frigate over her right shoulder. It was anchored in the near distance from the harbor.

A smile of pride lit his face. "Ah, there she is . . . The Brunswick."

Chapter 4

Sitting tranquilly anchored in the harbor was a British frigate with forty portholes for large metal cannons. It was a double-decked, fifth-rated sloop with an elegant modern hull designed expressly for speed. Even to Sarah's inexperienced eyes, the warship appeared to be outstandingly modern compared to the other larger vessels nearby.

The frigate's three masts stood tall and erect over the small Irish harbor. The mast to the right of the middle, known as the mizzen, was in the process of being repaired. A long piece of lumber, the size of a full-grown tree, was slowly being set in place

A crew of able-bodied seamen, she noticed, scrambled about on the top deck. An officer stood to one side barking out orders with the use of a brass, speaking trumpet. The men clambered agilely about the riggings making necessary repairs under the watchful eyes of the ship's master carpenter.

The sounds of hands at work, sawing and hammering, along with the strong smell of pitching tar, filled the air around the frigate. They slowly approached it on the much smaller Irish fishing craft.

When they reached its starboard side, an "Ahoy" was shouted up by Lieutenant Smythe.

An answering crewmember's head appeared over the stern. With a nod of greeting and the wave of a hand, the man acknowledged them. He disappeared from view and then lowered a wood seat suspended from two sturdy ropes, known as the baggy wrinkle.

The seaman clambered down the side to help them.

Robert greeted him with warm familiarity, handing over the small craft to be anchored. A hook was lowered and Sarah's small traveling chest was attached. The wood container held a few worldly possessions, bottled medicinal herbs and oils, the basic tools of her profession.

Warily, she eyed the suspended wood seat.

Although she knew how to swim, she nervously rubbed her arms. Afraid, her heart quailed inside her chest. She had visions of herself falling from the small seat into the cold sea below.

Oh, no. Please don't have them expect me to get into that flimsy contraption!

For a woman who had traveled through some of the most dangerous places in Ireland, she still had one great fear . . . she was afraid of heights. The irony wasn't lost on her. She'd been brought up on Varrik Island's lone, high hill. But she'd learned at an early age to hug the side of the dirt path, never looking down over the steep edge.

Gazing up the high, smooth side of the frigate made her queasy. The frigate was as tall as any church tower she'd ever seen. She realized how far up she was about to be dangled by the two ropes. She felt a lump of fear in her throat.

Noting her nervous expression, Robert said in reassuring tones, "'Tis perfectly safe, my dear. I'll be there beside you before your feet touch the deck."

The crewman looked up at the couple. A pleased smile spread across his tanned face. He tipped his hat at her.

"Excuse me for asking, sir . . . but are ye closely acquainted with the lovely lady, Lieutenant Smythe, sir?" he asked, staring with open approval, at the woman with shiny gold hair.

"Aye, Mr. Kelly. . . . I am so honored."

Carefully, he steadied her as she stood. His hands solicitously helped her into the baggy wrinkle. "This is my betrothed, Mistress Duncan. I'm bringing her home with me to England for our impending nuptials."

Without a word, he silently removed the Caddagh gold ring she wore on her right hand, turning the small band around then placing the ring back on. She was once again spoken for.

It tore a little at her heart. The ring, meant to be a symbol of love, was now being used as a ruse to help catch a murderous villain.

"If you are afraid, close your eyes on the way up. My men will see you safely aboard," he said. "Nothing bad will happen to you."

"Thank you," she managed to whisper.

He gave her hand a reassuring squeeze, signaling the crew to begin pulling her up. The pulley's wheels squeaked as they slowly moved her skyward.

Sarah felt a light sea breeze beneath her layers of wool skirts. They billowed out under her. The poignant sound of a flying seagull's cry echoed in the sky as it flew by. If she hadn't been so frightened, she would have opened her eyes and admired the view.

The Blasket Islands were dark green forms off in the near distance. They stood outlined in the hazy sunlight. Other boats, including light wooden framed currachs, small fishing boats covered in cowhide and painted with tar, were stacked on the shore. The small harbor dock of Dingle wasn't as crowded with fishing or merchant vessels as it used to be. The thriving community was currently more involved in the weaving trade.

Butterflies flitted about in her stomach. She kept her eyes firmly shut, while she held onto the thick, prickly ropes with a white-knuckled grip. She felt her body swing slightly. It was now suspended high over the bay's dark water.

The ropes ceased creaking. Strong hands reached out for her . . .

She felt herself being lifted up.

Once her feet touched the solid boards of the ship's deck, she let loose a breath of relief. She hadn't fallen. She was safely aboard.

Lieutenant Smythe swiftly climbed up the ship's rope ladder. He emerged between the thick bulwarks on the top deck. Gently, he held her as she accustomed herself to the ship's slight bobbing. She felt a warm tingling sensation of awareness course through her as his firm fingers touched her small waist.

His dark brown eyes looked down at her with concern.

"How are you feeling?" he asked.

"Fine." She smiled at him. She felt a tinge of blush creep into her cheeks. Her stomach did a small butterfly flip. It had been a long time since a man had showed any protective interest in her. It was pleasantly comforting and oddly natural.

A small whistle was blown, low, high, low. A seaman piped them aboard.

"Commander aboard, sir!" said a midshipman to an officer next to him.

Second in command, Lieutenant Litton's round, cherubic face presented itself. Doffing his hat respectfully, he gave a smart salute of welcome to his commander. He waited, as naval custom demanded, for his superior officer to speak first.

"Ah, Lieutenant Litton," Robert said, returning his salute. "I see she is no worse for wear from my absence. Aye, it would appear The Brunswick is becoming shipshape and seaworthy as per my orders."

"Aye, sir. Good to have you back aboard, sir," replied the technician as way of greeting. "And I see you've brought a guest with you, Commander."

"Ah, yes . . . Mr. Litton, I wish to present to you my betrothed, Mademoiselle Sarah Duncan. She is to be my special guest. I asked for her hand in marriage yesterday at her mother's home on Varrik Island. She has done me the great honor by accepting."

The other officer raised his eyebrows in a questioning manner at this shocking bit of news. Sarah could almost discern his thoughts.

Undoubtedly, he was wondering if the first mate had lost his mind. Perhaps even been bewitched by the Irish woman into proposing. For how did the lieutenant expect to ever be promoted by having such an unconventional bride?

She knew the second mate dared not question the officer.

The dark brown eyes that met the mate's inquiring watery blues were calm and detached. The commander's manner was as it should be—confident and aloof. The protective manner he exhibited towards Sarah warned Litton against saying anything unseemly about the lady standing beside him.

This Irish wise woman, despite her lowly social status, was now under the commander's protection. It would be suicidal to say anything careless. That is unless he was ready to cross swords with the seasoned lieutenant.

The second mate wisely kept silent.

Tipping his hat correctly in Sarah's direction, he quickly recovered his composure. He gave her a genuine smile of welcome and bowed politely over her outstretched hand.

"It is an honor to make your acquaintance, Mistress Duncan, ma'am . . . aye, a great pleasure indeed to have Commander Smythe's betrothed aboard."

Other officers, upon hearing this remark, gathered around.

[67]

Soft murmurs of appreciation over "the beauty," and conjecture of it being "love at first sight," were heard. Lower ranking, noncommissioned seamen nearby also observed the comely Irish colleen their master and commander had betrothed himself to.

"Will miracles never cease?" one of the ship's Irish gunners, a jolly man with red side whiskers, was heard to mutter. "It would appear that Lieutenant Smythe does have a beating heart after all."

"Aye, and who'd have thought Mister Chastity Belt capable of picking out such a winsomely pretty coo of a dove, eh?" added another. "Faith, the lass does have a very trim hull and a fine set o' rigging up front. Aye, the commander can easily lose himself in her."

A Scotsman added with a touch of salty, good humor, "And smooth skin a man would enjoy in his hammock—" The seaman broke off what he was about to say next under the stern, reprimanding glance of the second mate.

"That's enough of that, gentlemen. Return to your duties."

"Aye, aye, sir." The men nodded and hurried away.

Turning to Smythe, Litton asked, "Did Captain Jackson survive the journey, Commander? Did you find the healer you were seeking, sir?"

Hearing this question, the rest of the crew quieted. They listened intently to the reply of the first mate who'd taken full command of the frigate since the captain fell ill. The air about the men changed from frenzied activity to one of somber respect. They all wanted to know why Captain Jackson hadn't returned.

Robert shook his head sadly, removing his hat. He clasped his hands in front of him and bowed his head. He gave them the solemn news.

"Captain Jackson went on to his greater glory shortly after we landed on the island," he boldly lied, speaking loud enough so that all the crew nearby might hear his response. "We buried him there on the island—God rest his soul."

The crew took their hats off in respect. A few made the sign of the cross as they said a quiet prayer for the departed soul of their deceased captain.

"We will honor Captain Jackson's memory on the morrow with a short service, gentlemen," Robert said, taking full command of the ship.

He noted approvingly their solemn attitudes. Captain Jackson had been well liked. It was still difficult to believe that one of the crew had poisoned him.

"Aye, aye, sir," replied the men in unison.

* * *

Robert paged through his prayer book for the last rites of burial. There currently was no chaplain serving aboard. The fifth-rated warship was too small to merit one. As the ship's acting commander, he was expected to meet the spiritual needs of the crew. It was required of him to pay respects to the deceased with a proper burial service.

Other ships of the line had been known to undergo mutinies by unceremoniously dumping the dead into the sea. Without so much as a whisper of prayer to God for the soul of the departed, cold-hearted officers had thoughtlessly disposed of the deceased's body. Outraged by such callousness, ordinary seamen had been known to take arms on behalf of their departed shipmates.

Aye, he wanted to find the poisoning traitor as quickly as possible. He had to, before someone else became sick, or worse, dead.

"Mister Litton, I expect you to notify Master O' Grady's wife that I shall have need of her services as chaperone for my betrothed," he said. "Please, also inform the master carpenter and the other officers that I will wish to meet with them for an update of the ship's condition at the next bell."

"Aye, sir," the second mate replied.

He bowed slightly to Sarah and left on his errand.

She learned that there were two other ladies already living aboard The Brunswick. They were both standing officers' wives—the master gunner's and the master carpenter's. Only in peacetime were the captains of the Royal Navy permitted to bring their ladies aboard.

The lower ranking officers, the master gunner, boatswain, and carpenter received warrants from the navy. They were permanently attached to the same warship from the time she was first built until she fell apart or wrecked. It was not unusual, therefore, for their wives to come and live aboard with their husbands.

This was not however true of the superior officers, the captain and his lieutenants. They were assigned by commissions from the Royal Admiralty for a particular period of time. Their time of duty serving aboard a ship of the line could be anywhere from a matter of a few months to several years. Sometimes unassigned ranking officers waited around on tenterhooks on dry land, idly passing time in port gambling and wenching, not knowing when their next commission might be.

To a small degree, Sarah's presence aboard was setting a precedent. But as the frigate did not expect to see any fighting in friendly waters and currently was on its way back to their home port of Portsmouth, none of the other officers questioned it. It made sense that the first mate would wish to bring his pretty Irish bride back to England on his own vessel, rather than entrust her care to someone else.

Presenting his arm, Robert escorted her off the main, top deck up to the next level, the quarter deck. This part of the ship was considered to be the exclusive territory of the frigate's superior officers. No noncommissioned member of the crew touched a foot on this part of the ship, except when invited by a superior officer.

Looking around, she admired the beautiful lines of the sloop. She'd never been aboard a royal naval warship before. It was a new and exciting experience for a young woman who had been brought up on a small island.

She'd noted upon first seeing the frigate, the long white stripes which ran along the gun decks and under the painted black gun ports. Other white stripes ran up and down on each of the three tall sailing masts. The hull was painted black.

"Why are there white markings on the masts, Lieutenant?" she asked, curiously wondering at the decoration.

"They mark our frigate as fighting on the side of the British. That way none of our own warships will mistake us for the enemy and try to blow us out of the water."

"Oh," she said, much impressed.

She tried to imagine what it would be like to be in the middle of such a battle on this small vessel. "I can see how that might indeed be undesirable. But do tell me more about The Brunswick . . . are there many like her in the Royal Navy?"

"Aye, there are. And much has been made about the design of these frigates. The Royal Navy is busy having their top designers build an entire fleet of them," he said proudly.

"The speed and the agility of this fifth-rated ship-of-the-line are enviable. She and her kind can do what no other larger vessel can. She is able to quickly maneuver through the sea at a brisk speed of twelve knots. Although heavily sailed, she can surprisingly turn nimbly about. She is much faster compared to the larger warships of the fleet."

"Indeed . . ." Sarah breathed, looking up once more at the tall masts before her.

"Aye, these frigates are considered to be 'the eyes of the fleet.' They are capable of acting as efficient messengers. They can swiftly slip between enemy lines, harassing larger first-rated warships and giving support to other vessels blocking important seaports. But they do have one weakness . . ."

"And what would that be?" she asked.

"She's vulnerable to being pulverized. If attacked by better-armed enemy warships, she will be nothing but splintered wood bits . . . aye, a larger vessel with its multitude of cannons can easily dispatch us to the high heavens by simply blasting us out of the water."

"She is nonetheless a grand warship," said Sarah, pleased to be standing aboard the most modern vessel in the entire Royal Navy.

She could not help but think of the great Lord Admiral Nelson, who when asked by a reporter what he wanted for the Royal Navy, replied, "More frigates, sir! More frigates! If I were to die this moment, 'want of frigates' would be found engraved upon my heart."

And here she was, a simple, wise woman from Ireland, standing on the quarter-deck of one of the finest warships ever built. It was truly an honor.

* * *

He led her down to his first mate's living quarters located on the lower middle deck. It was a small room situated next to what the seamen called "the captain's great cabin." The cabin was built in the stern at the frigate's protruding end. Robert had not felt comfortable taking over Captain Jackson's living quarters. It remained unoccupied.

The first mate's cabin next door was tight and cramped. However, it was spacious and private by comparison to the noncommissioned seamen's. The crew's dormitory styled quarters were situated on the opposite end of the deck.

He intended on installing her in his quarters. He would rig a hammock tonight in the nearby wardroom where the lower ranking officers slept. Not a finger's breadth of space was wasted on the frigate.

Upon entering the small first mate's cabin, she tried to squeeze past Robert to hang up her bonnet on a nearby hook. He turned with his hands full of his own belongings, but a sudden swell from the ocean caught her off balance. Before anyone could say, "Redcoats are red roosters," Sarah stumbled against him, pushing him backwards onto the narrow cabin bed.

"Oh," she murmured under her breath as she landed safely on top of him, his firm hands went around her waist as he dropped his belongings in a futile effort to keep her steady.

Her breasts were pressed up against his chest as she found herself mere inches from his mouth. She could feel his warm breath upon her skin. Looking into his dark eyes, she saw her reflection and with some embarrassment realized her ample bosom now took up a good portion of his view. As if mesmerized, they continued to stare into each other's eyes.

For a brief moment, Sarah wondered what it would be like to be kissed by him. Would his lips be soft against hers or hard and demanding? And the very thought of such a kiss set her heart pounding.

"Um . . . ," said Robert with some belabored breathing. "I do believe it would be for the best if you got off me now, Mistress ."

"Oh, of course," she said, her eyes never leaving his. Cheeks flaming, she pulled herself up to a sitting position next to him. Her hands shook a little as she patted a loose hair back into place.

It'd been over a year since she'd been this close to a man. She'd loved her late fiancé, the burly John Maxwell, and they had planned to marry upon his return from service. She'd enjoyed their lovemaking, deciding waiting was unnecessary, as they'd been committed to each other. Now the handsome master and commander had reawakened all the emotions she'd kept pent-up inside her body, by accidentally pressing his body against hers.

Heavens, it's a good thing he cannot read my thoughts, for sure now they are not that of a proper gentlewoman's. Indeed, as she lifted a hand to feel her heated cheeks, it was quite the opposite.

Gathering his things, he hurriedly prepared to leave the cabin.

"Shall I give you a couple of minutes to tidy yourself and then return to escort you to the captain's cabin where we shall take a look at his personal log?" he inquired before leaving.

"Yes," she said, nodding, while adjusting the lace fichu, which had slipped off to one side of her bodice during their encounter. He turned and left, giving her the time she needed to cool the flames that burned her cheeks.

* * *

A red, uniformed marine saluted them outside the captain's cabin.

Robert smartly returned it and they entered. Captain Jackson had given him advanced permission to look into his personal log, a document separate from The Brunswick's.

He sighed deeply upon opening the door. His face

was dark with troubled thoughts of what he was about to undertake as the first mate. The upcoming days would decide not just Captain Jackson's future, but his, as well.

"What is troubling you?" she asked, noting his expression.

"My every action from here on in will be minutely scrutinized by the Royal Admiralty," he confessed. "A single blameworthy error on my part could end any hopes I may have entertained of ever being promoted to the rank of captain. Indeed it may occasion something much worse."

He prudently closed the door behind them. There was no need for the sentry to overhear their conversation and possibly report it to the other hands.

"If Captain Jackson should decide to find fault with what I do during this time of his convalescence, he may have me brought before a naval tribunal and court-martialed for any incompetence, real or imagined. I am now walking a fine line between safety and an open, damning abyss."

"You are doing right by taking command. Captain Jackson could not have done so, even if he were here right now. He could barely sit up and speak when we left him. You still would have been forced to take his place, as undoubtedly you did before. Nay, 'tis right. You've no other choice. You must proceed as planned."

"Aye, although this is not how I hoped our voyage to your mother's island would end," he agreed. Resolutely, he walked over to the captain's desk.

He opened the log.

It was encased in a leather cover. The parchments inside were smeared by Indian ink. The tobacco Captain Jackson smoked smelled pungently from the opened pages. Reading, Robert looked them over.

"There is little here to point us in the direction as to who may have been trying to kill him. Everything appears to have been normal. No malicious notes of discontent from any of the men, no heated arguments with the officers, just the everyday discipline of normal routine. The only evidence that points to anything out of the ordinary is this entry here . . ."

He fingered the page before him.

"Captain Jackson began to admit to not feeling well. It was shortly after we brought the captured French warship, La Bonne Chance, back to England."

"'When was that?'"

"One week later," he said, looking again at the entry in which the captain began to admit to 'not feeling quite up to scratch.'

"We were fair proud of ourselves, almost bursting out of our britches at having captured a blockade runner. It was the second one in two years we had managed to nab. The first had been of Spanish origin, a small fifth-rated vessel. But this one, this one was particularly special. She was a French merchant's cargo ship. Aye, a real beauty, she was—expressly made for smuggling black-market goods. And it was we who had the good fortune that day."

His face lit with pride.

He remembered the capture . . . it had been difficult wrestling away the vessel from the blockade runners. In the end, as the ship surrendered, the captain of La Belle Chance shot himself, choosing to die rather than be imprisoned.

Robert had often asked himself what he would have done if the situation had been reversed. Instead of being captured and clapped in irons, would he too have taken his own life? He did not know . . . he recognized he would not know until such an event occurred. Happily, so far, it had not.

"By way of celebration, Captain Jackson gave the officers shore leave. The married men sent for their wives and the rest of the crew took to drinking themselves senseless."

He smiled. "Captain Jackson and I visited some of the finest taverns in town for food and entertainment. It was a good time . . . shortly thereafter, he fell ill."

"How long after was it?"

"One week," he answered. "Aye, ill winds seem to have followed us ever since the day we captured La Belle Chance. It would appear we cannot shake it."

"Were there any new hands who signed on at that time?"

He nodded in thought. He then looked through the enlistment roll, the sheet the hands marked when joining the ship's crew. Slowly, he shook his head. There appeared to be nothing of value to be found in the logs.

"His servant had been with him already for six months and the cook for over a year," he said, closing the book as a bell tolled the hour. "There were, however, three men who enlisted after we captured La Belle Chance . . . a young noncommissioned seaman, a gunner, and a marine. It does not appear that any of these men would have gained anything by the captain's death."

"So it would seem," she agreed, wondering what motive lay behind the assassin's attempt to end the captain's life.

What had prompted this villain to try and kill the captain on his own vessel? In these tight quarters, it would be difficult to go unnoticed. How had he managed to sneak the poison into the captain's food?

Robert stood up from the table, closing the log.

He carefully put it back in its original place. When Captain Jackson returned, everything would be as he left it. The ship's bell tolled. It was time to hear about the progress made in repairing the ship during his short absence.

"I have a meeting with Lieutenant Litton and the

other officers, and therefore, I must excuse myself."

Catching a whiff of lavender and sea salt permeating from the wise woman, he felt reluctant to leave. If it were not for the fact that he had duties to perform, he would be tempted to spend more time in her company. Recalling the feel of her luscious curves when she fell against him earlier reminded him just how long he'd been without a woman. Aye, she was a beauty to be sure, as well as charming and intelligent. She was also here for a serious purpose, he sternly reminded himself.

He cleared his throat, needing to get back to the matter at hand.

"While I meet with Mr. Litton in the wardroom, perhaps you would like to rest or visit the rest of The Brunswick with one of our young seamen as an escort?"

"I would enjoy viewing her." She smiled, her face aglow with excitement.

He cleared his throat again. "Excellent. Remain here and I'll send one of the crew to escort you about." He beat a hasty retreat, feeling hot blood rushing to heat his loins. Outside the door, he took a deep, calming breath. He needed to get a hold of himself. He was behaving like an untried youth and not like an acting captain of one of his majesty's finest warships.

"The devil take it, man!" he told himself. "Get a hold of yourself!" Briskly, he walked away from temptation's door and went to the officers' meeting.

Chapter 5

Shortly after Robert left, she heard a knock on the cabin door. Sarah opened it and found a young seaman about her height and size, standing there. It was difficult to discern his age. The face seemed more mature than that of a young boy. But he did not have the square masculine features of a grown man.

The seaman wore the usual uniform of a common sailor. He sported a loose white shirt, a red wool jacket, and baggy trousers, with a red-checkered handkerchief tied around his neck. His curly dark black hair was worn in a neat pigtail in the back. On the whole, the lad appeared to be sturdily built. He was, as she was to describe him later, a pretty youth.

Wide, brown eyes looked her up and down appraisingly. She wore the blue, homespun gown her mother had helped her sew with inset laced sleeves. The young man's sherry-colored eyes focused their inspection, first on her face, taking in her fair porcelain features, unblinkingly gazing into her light blue eyes. He then looked upwards to her gold-colored hair.

But what he did next surprised her . . . his assessing eyes traveled back down to her bosom. The lad stared boldly at the lace lining of her tightly fitted bodice where the globes of her breasts peeped modestly out of the empire-styled bodice. The Irish lace lining the garment demurely screened her bosom from full view and was tucked back in its proper place.

She felt herself growing angry under his insolent regard. Did he know what had transpired in Robert's cabin, and if so, what business was it of his?

Sarah's sapphire-blue eyes gleamed with anger. This lad was boldly staring at her chest . . . what the devil did he think he was about? She was not some harbor trollop to be stared at in such an insolent way!

On the verge of setting the impudent lad properly in his place by giving him a good facer with the flat of her hand, she watched as his manner suddenly changed. It was as if the young seamen suddenly remembered who she was.

He bowed and presented himself to her in a correct, deferential manner, as befitted her station as the commanding officer's future bride.

"I'm Jeremy, ma'am," he said in a soft voice, giving her a curious look. "Lieutenant Smythe asked me to escort you about. He said you wanted to become more familiar with The Brunswick, ma'am."

"That's correct, seaman," she said in frigid tones, letting him know of her displeasure at his open familiarity. She drew the paisley shawl more closely about her.

Fervently, she wished that it were the first mate showing her about the frigate, not this wee bit of puffed up manhood. There was something not correct about the young seaman's attitude towards her.

Aye, she could not quite put her finger on it. Something was definitely amiss. Her intuition told her that something was not quite right with this lad.

She knew Jeremy did not hold her in any kind of respect. His raking look upon first meeting had not held the deference due her as either a lady or as the fiancée of the highest ranking officer aboard. It had been openly insolent and cold.

But why was the lad behaving so badly? Why was

he speaking to her with barely veiled contempt? It was as if he knew her betrothal to Lieutenant Smythe to be all but a sham. Was the little imp secretly mocking her?

Despite the young sailor's now seemingly polite manners, the uneasiness she felt upon first meeting him did not diminish as he escorted her about.

Following Jeremy, she descended two decks to the bottom of the frigate, the cargo hull. It was here that repair materials were kept. Most of the crew was outside finishing their duties. It was empty of any other human presence.

She had been on other sloops before with her godfather, Duncan, the fisherman who had pulled her out of the sea as a baby, but this naval warship was almost twice as large as any fishing vessel. It was also impeccably clean and shipshape.

The brass shone in the waning afternoon light. The wood decks were well swabbed, sanded, and cared for with several coatings of lemon and wax. The inexperienced seamen, not yet ranked as able-bodied, had been on their hands and knees, moving back and forth across the planks with book-sized pieces of sandstone. The end result of their labor being that the wood now gleamed from the sanding.

Jeremy led her down past the berth deck.

The familiar smell of livestock assailed her senses. A mixture of hay, gunpowder, manure, and a variety of other smells she associated with small, tenant farms, assaulted her nose. This area was where the officers penned their livestock of chickens, pigs, goats, and cows, next to the guns and cannons.

There were other animals aboard with the livestock, she noted. The crew was permitted to keep pets. Occasionally, she heard the squawking of parrots and the loud bark of a dog. A few cats also freely prowled around, working for their keep. They kept the population of the ship's rats down.

They descended farther. She knew when they reached the bottom level of the frigate. Her skin prickled with anticipation. Small, unseen brown and black vermin with long tails hid there.

Pairs of dark, beady eyes stared out from the top of cargo boxes. She could hear tiny feet scurry away at their approach.

Shivering, she tightened her grip on her paisley shawl. Rodents were not one of her preferred creatures. She had never intended to descend this far down. But Jeremy had adamantly insisted on including it on the tour.

She noted baited pieces of bread soaked in arsenic lying about. She'd been told the poison was kept locked in the captain's trunk and put out for these small vermin. It might have been how the assassin obtained his.

The young seaman paused at the hull's hatch door. He took a candle down from a stand and lit it. He led her arm, firmly gripping her elbow.

Ouch—his hold hurt.

"Take your hand off of me!" she snapped.

"You want to see all of the ship, don't you, ma'am?" Jeremy asked, his tone oily. "The commander told me to let you explore every inch of her, Mistress Duncan. You're not afraid, are ye, ma'am?"

She gave him a frosty stare, clearly indicating that she had no desire to go any further. He would have to drag her down first. At the same time a horrible stench assailed her senses. She wrinkled her nose. The smell came from the frigate's bilge water.

Merciful heavens, it's horribly foul! She pinched her nose. *That green slime on the floor of the hull . . . is that what's making the dreadful stink? If so, I am not going to take another step.*

Jeremy smirked at her look of disgust.

"I thought an Irish lady brought up on a remote island, such as yourself, ma'am, would want to see all of the grand ship that your future husband is in charge of. Especially seeing how poor Captain Jackson is dead . . . God keep his soul."

Does he want me to contradict him? If Jeremy desired her to tell him that Captain Jackson wasn't dead, but actually still alive, and therefore the tour of the hull quite unnecessary, she almost obliged.

But instead of setting her tongue loose, she held it. She detested the idea of letting this inflated wee bit of jackanapes see her afraid.

Is he trying to unnerve me on purpose? Does he think I'm not worthy of becoming the first mate's wife? She was full of indignation. *And if so, who the devil does he think he is to judge me?*

She stiffened her spine. *Faith, I'll show this forward scamp of a boy that I'm made of far sterner stuff than bits of petticoat and lace. I am as strong as any English lady!*

Poised to open her mouth and order him to take her directly back up to the top deck, something happened that caused her heart to pound with genuine fear. It killed the sharp words poised on the tip of her tongue, silencing them forever.

The candle guttered out . . . she stood alone in complete darkness.

Disoriented, she realized the hand that had been pulling her forcefully down into the bowels of the ship, suddenly disappeared. Instinctively, she reached out, her fingers grasping at nothing but air. However, it did not remain dark for long.

* * *

Later, Sarah tried to describe it to Robert as they dined alone in the wardroom that night. In the safety of the quiet cabin room, she felt as if it were someone else who had lived the events she was retelling.

The best she could do was say, "It was as dark as tar down there. I could not see my own hand. I felt a sudden chill in the air about us and everything was unnaturally quiet."

Goose pimples ran along her arms as she recalled the frightening moment.

"The hair on the back of my neck rose. I sensed . . . nay, I knew, something or someone was standing behind me. Then I turned and saw . . . ," she paused, taking a healthy swallow of sherry, "a ghost."

"You saw a what?"

"It was a pale ball of light at first, floating next to the cargo boxes. It slowly took a form, turning into something more solid and recognizable. First, a head . . . followed by shoulders . . . and then finally the rest of the spirit's body."

"What did this ghost look like?"

"He looked like a dead seaman."

When the unearthly apparition materialized in front of her, she had almost leapt with fear. The hull had suddenly turned bone cold. Her breath came out in small, white puffs of air.

"Anything else?" he asked, eyeing her across the candlelit table. "Did it indicate who it might be? What it might want?"

"It was wrapped in what appeared to be long strands of seaweed. It lifted pale arms and pointed an accusing finger at Jeremy . . ." She knit her brows together in an endeavor to remember exactly what followed.

"My heart was thumping so hard. Yet I could not let loose a scream. It stayed lodged in the back of my throat. I was terrified, unable to move. Fear held me in place as strongly as any tight rope."

"How did Jeremy react to this specter?" He leaned closer. Sarah's voice had descended to a barely audible whisper.

"He fainted dead away," she recalled. "His lamp

dropped out of his hands." Shaking with fright, she had had the courage to pick it up. Almost slipping in her haste, she had turned back to the tinder box by the hatch.

"I managed to light the candle and proceeded to come back down to confront the specter. But before I had an opportunity to speak, to ask what it wanted . . . it vanished."

"Then what did you do?"

"I checked on Jeremy. I was beginning to loosen his neck cloth when he came to. He looked about, startled at first. Then he sat up and did something I would never in the world have imagined."

"Which was?"

"He laughed, Lieutenant . . . he chuckled with uncontrolled delight. It was as if the ghost's strange appearance had been nothing but a bit of tomfoolery. Apparently, the sole purpose of this was to frighten me."

"Never!"

"Aye," she said, nodding in agreement.

She still was not quite certain herself as to why the seaman had reacted that way. "It was then he informed me of the truth of what had just taken place."

"Which was?"

"That he had asked one of his shipmates to hide behind the cargo boxes and dress himself up as a ghost, covering himself in white flour and seaweed. Another had taken a magic lantern and made a pin prick of light to appear and disappear, or so he said. He laughed and told me that it had all been a prank to baptize me into life aboard ship. An initiation, he said it was."

"Did you believe him?" Robert scowled, upset on the wise woman's behalf.

The lad should never have taken her down to the cargo hull. It was not a suitable place for any visitor aboard the ship, and most certainly not a lady. He was prepared to summon the young seaman to his side for a brutal face-to-face with the nearest judgment from God—a moment alone with his angry acting commander.

"Nay," she said calmly.

Jeremy's joviality had been forced. She had sensed it. But why pretend? And where were these so called other pranksters? Why was it the young seaman had been the only one standing there laughing?

"It all felt quite false, a veritable farce put forth by one person. I did not believe what he told me for an instant. It was pure blarney," she finished.

The first mate's frown deepened. He disliked these shenanigans. The dark image of a ghost suddenly appearing out of nowhere made him uncomfortable. Added to that, when he thought of the lovely wise woman in possible danger, he was ready to enact martial law. If she'd been harmed in any way, he'd have wrung the lad's neck with his own bare hands. Gripping his chair in anger, he decided the impudent sailor and his co-conspirators were about to pay dearly for their nasty prank.

"I'll have him and his mates put in the brig for this," he muttered.

He felt his authority was being questioned by making a mockery of the beautiful woman under his protection. "But before I do that, I'll flog the prankster myself! How dare the little bugger . . . the rascal, I'll make him sorely regret his actions."

"No, don't!" she said, placing a restraining hand on him. "I don't want any difficulties because of this foolishness. The crew has been through a terrible time with the loss of one of their shipmates, the fire, and now their captain's announced death. They have had everything thrown at them at once. 'Tis acceptable with me if I am the one to make them laugh, to ease the tension . . . there's no need to punish anyone. No harm has come to either me or to the ship. Aye, there is no need to exact any revenge on my behalf."

She had personally taken care of that.

What she did not add to her tale was the fact that after the young seaman confessed what he'd done, she slapped him angrily across the face and then had promptly gone directly back up to the berth deck.

Once out of the hull, she began pulling a heavy potato sack across the trap door. She had some help. Master O'Grady, the master gunner, who upon seeing her struggle with the heavy sack, unquestioningly aided her.

She sat down on it. Calmly, she ignored the poundings and urgent shouts emitting from the other side. Blithely she smiled like a queen on her throne, at the seamen gathered about.

"I hope ye won't take offense if I was to be asking if ye be in fair weather, ma'am?" asked the burly Irish gunner.

Frantic thumping sounds emanated from the sack beneath her.

"I'm desirous to do a bit of sitting, Mr. O' Grady. That's all I'm doing." She smiled up at him and the other hands. "I'm afraid a wee bit of respect is needed to be taught to a certain young seaman aboard this warship."

"For sure, ma'am," said the Irishman mildly. "May I be so bold as to ask which one of our unworthy lads that would be, Mistress Duncan? Who needs the reprimanding?"

"A certain Jeremy Kaye by name, sir," she said with a small offended sniff. "He was supposed to escort me about The Brunswick. Instead, he took me on a trip down to Hades itself."

"Did that undisciplined, English buffoon offend your tender Celtic sensibilities, ma'am?" asked the Irish gunner, flexing an arm the size of a sturdy log.

"Would you like me to teach him what we sons of

Erin do to those who give a pretty colleen, such as yourself, trouble?" asked another.

The other men gathered about her beamed eager smiles of agreement down at the flaxen-haired beauty. Aye, they muttered in agreement, they would all like to have a hand in punishing the young upstart. How dare the little braggart treat the commander's betrothed this way! How dare he mock her!

"It would be delightful to give the young sea pup a proper paddling, especially when the lad is such a stuck up little bugger," continued Mr. O' Grady.

A chorus of rough 'ayes' were heard from the other able-bodied seamen.

"Nay, nay, gentlemen." She beamed, rearranging her skirts prettily about her. "No need to go concerning yourselves over this small matter. I'm perfectly content to sit here and let the bilge rat remain in his rightful hiding place."

She was happy . . . her revenge was complete.

Jeremy and his fellow pranksters, if there were any others, were down in the dark hull. They were unable to stir up any further trouble. Only when the steward came to fetch her for the evening meal with Robert, did she finally relinquish her makeshift throne. Master O'Grady, his wife, and various other members of the crew, pressed her to let them take her place.

"We'd be honored," they said, "to stand guard for ye, ma'am."

Before she could say, "Jack your brother," more than half the hands volunteered. It would be well into the next day before the seaman was released.

Nay, I do not need to worry about what happened in the hull. There's no need for the first mate to do any bloodletting on my behalf. The crew has seen to that.

Chapter 6

They finished their dinner pleasantly discussing places they both had visited. They talked about the various journeys they had taken, including the people they'd met. To Robert's surprise, he learned that the wise woman was used to associating with those above her station. He noted during their conversation that there were times when she spoke with mocking humor about those considered to be her betters. He liked her all the more for it.

Secretly, he was impressed by the way she handled herself in his company. Most women of his acquaintance were a bit overawed by his presence and tended to babble on about mundane inanities, as if a commanding officer could possibly care that their dancing instructor didn't know any French or that their mother wouldn't let them wear wetted gowns to a ball. Other ladies paled, as well, when compared to Sarah's natural beauty and feminine charm, which he found to be most alluring and innocently exciting. Indeed, he had never met a woman like her.

He himself had not been raised among the upper crust. Having earned his rank as a first lieutenant through merit, he felt uncomfortable among those who did not. The Smythe family's origins were from among the solid merchant class. He did not aspire to a title higher than that of a captain of the Royal Navy. Although he knew of five naval admirals who had risen up the ranks this way, his aspirations did not lead him in that direction. He wanted simply to be in command of a naval warship.

"Do you play any instruments?" he asked. Her blonde eyelashes, he noted, were very long and her mouth as she smiled at him, was generous, just right for kissing, he mused.

She shook her head. "I enjoy it. But the best I can do is sing a little. Being brought up on a remote island never provided me with the opportunity. And you, do you play any instruments, Lieutenant?"

"I was most fortunate as a lad—I served on second and first rated warships as a young midshipman. They had several talented musicians. Under the tutelage of two of the chaplains, I learned to play a little of the harpsichord and mandolin."

She smiled, looking about to see if any instruments were available "Will you not play for me now? It's been a long time since I heard any melodies. When I was young, my mother would sometimes play on a penny whistle for me. Sometimes," she modestly confessed, "I'm invited to my friend Lady Beatrice's evening concerts at Brightwood Manor. My voice, it may be supposed, cannot be too out of tune. She often asks me to sing."

"If that is true, I must see what I can do to fulfill your wish. Give me one moment," he said, "and we shall have our own little musical soiree. I should be delighted to hear what a sweet voice you've been blessed with."

He held himself back from adding that if her voice matched the rest of her appearance, he was in for a treat. Instead, he excused himself and went in search of the instrument.

Bearing the mandolin carefully in his hands, he returned.

He took it out of its case and placed it upon his knee. She noticed how strong and wide his thighs were, like the beams of the ship, sturdy, perfect for sitting on.

Before long they were singing in unison. Merry melodies that were familiar to both of them were heard echoing out the cabin window onto the bay. On some of the slower songs, his deep baritone joined her light soprano. The two voices blended together in perfect tune and pitch, encouraging the other to sing on.

He enjoyed watching her luscious mouth as she sang, the light of enjoyment in her light blue eyes. Sometimes her voluptuous bosom swelled upwards as she took in a deep breath, and he was forced to gaze elsewhere to keep from gawking at her like a school boy.

He had no right to think of touching the lovely Irish woman. She was under his protection. *She trusts you,* he sternly reminded himself. *Don't be a cad and ruin it by giving into your carnal desires.*

Observing him opened the wise woman's eyes to a different aspect of his character. The minute he held the instrument in his hands, cradling it in the same competent manner he did his sexton, his whole demeanor changed. All the tenseness he held on his stiff uniformed shoulders during the day dropped away.

Music indeed can lighten a man's burden.

He appeared more relaxed and content, lifting the corner of his mouth into a genuine warm smile. Something she had not seen since they'd come aboard. He always appeared to be in firm command of himself and those around him, except now, when playing.

Her feet lightly tapped the boards in time to the music as they went through a rollicking rendition of *Whiskey in the Rye.*

In the future, when we dine together, I shall make a point of asking him to play. For surely it must do him some good to set aside his burdens as commander of this fine ship for a little while.

Watching him made her aware of the way he always held himself in check. He was always in tight control. His duty as acting captain, she understood, was both a blessing and a burden. But he had met the challenge of taking over for Captain Jackson admirably. He had done so with self-assurance, knowing he was able to command both the ship and the crew. There had been no doubts. And she respected and admired him because of it.

As she watched him play, she couldn't help but notice his long, muscular arms, and idly wondered if he could hold a woman as well as he could an instrument? Undoubtedly, it would be most enjoyable to find out, she decided, gazing up at him from beneath her lashes. She then berated herself for thinking such wicked thoughts, for who was she but a lowly Irish wise woman. *He will want someone of higher rank than you. Stop behaving like a moonstruck schoolgirl around him and be of good use instead.*

She vowed to do what she could to help him, to see if she could make his life more agreeable. Maybe she could give the cook a hand with the food? She thought tasting the almost bland food placed in front of her. Perhaps help the other women aboard with their work . . . surely she could be of some use during her time aboard.

Thus resolved, she smiled up at him and enjoyed the rest of the evening in his company. For a few happy moments she forgot the awful events that had frightened her witless earlier. She put them aside and relaxed in his safe company. But unfortunately that evening was not to be the end of the matter between her, Jeremy Kaye, and the ghost. It was merely the beginning.

* * *

Lieutenant Smythe, upon retiring for the night, encountered the rather unusual watch being held on top of the potato sack. Upon learning why the master carpenter's wife, Mistress Kelly, was perched there, he insisted on having a turn.

When the crew passed the hatch on their way to their hammocks that night they were greeted by a rather odd sight . . . their commanding officer was seated on a rustic gunny sack.

He softly whistled a well-known sea shanty, while whittling on a piece of driftwood. They quietly saluted him, tipping their hats as they passed.

"Night, Lieutenant Smythe," they said as they passed to their hammocks.

Robert nodded politely in turn, acting as if this were a perfectly normal way for him, the master and commander of one of the swiftest warships of the line, to pass his free time.

His men appreciated his loyalty to his betrothed. They were glad to be serving under a gentleman with such discerning taste. Many of them, including several of the officers, envied him his choice of bride. For the beautiful Irish woman had proven she was not a spineless petticoat. She was a grand lady, worthy of their respect.

* * *

The morning of the memorial service for Captain Jackson was a somber affair. Sarah watched Robert give the eulogy from the quarter-deck. She looked about for Jeremy. Her nemesis was noticeably absent. He was nowhere to be seen.

Perhaps he had gone back to his bunk or been placed in the brig? Either way, she was secretly relieved she did not have to face him. She wanted to concentrate on the service, not on his unwelcome presence.

At the end of the memorial, Robert solemnly

intoned, "Deal graciously, O' Lord, we pray, with all who mourn this day. We cast all care on you, that we may know the consolation of your love through Jesus Christ our Lord. Amen."

They sang a hymn as Mrs. Kelly played the small organ kept in the corner of the lower deck for Sunday services. Robert turned to Mr. Litton and nodded in a familiar signal known to both from years of working together.

"Crew . . . diss-missed!" the second mate said in a commanding voice that carried to those on the lower deck.

The men quickly dispersed, returning to their assigned duties.

Sarah looked again for Jeremy, wondering what had become of him. She knew that Lieutenant Smythe had kept his promise not to have the seaman punished because the boatswain, the officer in charge of superintending such punishments, had not been summoned.

Later that afternoon she learned why she had not seen him. The simple reason was that he was no longer aboard.

The young seaman had spent twenty-four hours trapped in the stinking hull. Upon being released, he was given his morning mess and confined to quarters. But instead of attending the morning memorial service for Captain Jackson, the lad had taken the opportunity to slip overboard and swim for shore. Unseen by the rest of the crew who were busy attending the memorial service, he escaped.

The ship's Marines and a small longboat crew were sent ashore to track down and find the wayward deserter. But not a trace of him was to be found. Jeremy had apparently found means in which to quickly escape the harbor. He was now out of their reach.

"I should have had him shackled in irons," Robert

said, upon learning of the sailor's escape, "and properly flogged. A little bloodletting would have certainly impeded his escape. I assumed the lad had learned his lesson and would reform his ways. More the fool I!"

Miserably, she conceded, "It is undoubtedly my fault, Lieutenant Smythe. I am most sorry for it. If you had not listened to me, he would not now be gone. I hope the Royal Admiralty does not blame you for this sorry affair. If they do utter a word against you because of this, please place all the blame on my shoulders. I am, after all, the featherbrained female who thought he would act honorably after you dealt him so mild a punishment."

He smiled at her, his anger quickly disappearing.

The wise woman's face was contrite and repentant. She was quite becoming in the morning sunlight, standing next to him on the quarter-deck. She wore a simple dove gray morning gown. Her gold locks of hair peeked out in curled tendrils from under her plain straw bonnet. She had beribboned it appropriately with black velvet for the memorial.

He consoled her. "You are not to blame, Mistress Duncan. Neither one of us could have possibly known how Jeremy would react. Truth be told, this is the only second desertion The Brunswick has had in the past two years. It is an admirable record most captains would envy. Nay, the Admiralty will say nothing about this regrettable event."

"Men desert that frequently, sir?"

"Aye, I'm afraid so," he answered truthfully. "Those pressed into service, the homesick, and those disillusioned about life at sea, will on occasion jump ship. Aye, I am afraid it is a common enough event. One unfortunately a captain of a man-of-war must come to expect in these uncertain times. Loyalty to king and country can mean much, or for some very little."

"And the hands, will they miss Jeremy greatly? Have I deprived you of an important member of your crew?"

"Nay. Jeremy was a capable enough foretop man," he said, referring to the sailors who were assigned to the highest part of the ship's tall masts. They worked rigging the sails, serving on watch, and acting as marksmen in battle, firing from the maintops at any invading intruders trying to board the ship.

"But he was not so indispensable a seaman that I could not easily replace him with another. From what I understand, he was not particularly well liked by a great number of the hands. Therefore, he shall not in the least be missed. Apparently, the lad had no friends. He kept to himself, believing himself somehow to be superior to the others. Aye, a true loner was our wayward sailor."

He took her hand comfortingly into his own.

"Do not trouble yourself on his account, Mistress Duncan. To dwell on the matter, my dear, will only give you cause to frown. As the commander of this vessel, I must say it would displease me greatly to see you thus."

He daringly kissed her hand.

It was a gentle and tender gesture, one she had cause to dwell upon with a contented smile on her face for the rest of the day. The sight of the proud and proper commanding Lieutenant Smythe bending over her was endearing. He had been more than kind. He had managed to abate all the secret fears she had guiltily held concerning her part in Jeremy's decision to desert.

She would have gladly swept the matter cleanly from her thoughts, as he had recommended, but that was not to be. A darker event was about to overshadow the others.

*   *   *

As the sun reached its zenith the next day, an excitable gentleman in a long black overcoat came running up the gangplank, bringing word of a most unusual find. A dead body had been recovered from the sea.

Robert recognized the excitable gentleman as being the local constable of Dingle Harbor. The local Irish called him their *Garda Siochanca*. He went and greeted the man thinking that perhaps Jeremy may have been found.

That morning he had filed a report with the constable of the port about the sailor's disappearance. In return he had been assured that the town's officials would spread the word around to keep an eye out for the young deserter.

But instead of bringing word about Jeremy's whereabouts, the Garda brought the disturbing news of a retrieved dead body. It had recently washed ashore on a remote part of the southern peninsula not far from Dingle.

"A shepherd from Lipspole sighted the body snagged on a bit of seaweed. We rowed out and fetched it. He had come in on a high tide, Commander."

"Do you have any idea as to the man's identity?"

"Nay, not a wit . . . but what clothes the dead man wore were of a noticeable nature. He still wore a knit sweater with a distinctive pattern. I'm up and asking all the captains around the harbor t' take a proper look at the body in case he be a lost member of their crew," said the ruddy faced Irishman.

He regarded Robert in a man-to-man fashion. He confided, "There have been a few good seamen gone missing these last few days because of the recent gales. I heard tell yours had lost a hand, and I must confess that this is not the only reason why I wish ye to take a look at him . . ." He hesitated, as if he were not certain he should continue.

"What else?"

Sarah could feel the hairs on the back of her neck prickle with anticipation. She second-guessed the reason why the town's constable wanted him to see the body. Something was not right about the death.

The constable glanced at them, as if weighing whether or not they were worthy of his confidences. They were not members of the small close-knit community. Could this English commander be trusted?

At last he nodded and said, "The death was not natural. He was found with a whalebone dagger firmly stuck in his back. Well planted, it was, right between his ribs. It was deliberately forced into him. The blade skewered one of his ribs, splitting cleanly in half, undoubtedly touching his heart and killing him. It was done with evil intent. Murder it was, sir."

He took out a long stemmed clay dhudeen pipe from his coat and sucked on it thoughtfully. He pointed the stem of it at Robert. His face was grim with concern.

"Aye, I do not envy the man who can identify him, Commander," he said, "for he'll have the devil's own responsibility of cleaning up the mess and dealing out the dead man's vengeance. Aye, that can be particularly unsavory. Especially if the murderer be found to be a member of his own crew."

The constable gave the newly appointed master and commander a thoughtful look. He had heard of how the first mate had been forced to take over command of The Brunswick because of Captain Jackson's sudden death.

By the speculative look he gave the young commander, Sarah could tell he was wondering if the English officer was up to the task of taking control of such a mercurial situation.

Seamen were a hotheaded, superstitious lot. Even the militarily disciplined ones were known for their brash, unthinking behavior when pressed into an unyielding corner. How would the unseasoned commander handle the situation if the dead seaman proved to be one of his own men? Would he do his duty and go after the perpetrator?

"Not every man has the stomach to deal with such bothersome troubles," the constable said aloud. "Nasty business all this is, Commander. Nasty."

"Where has the body been laid?" asked Robert, catching the eye of the second mate, who stood next to them intently listening to the conversation.

"We placed it with the village's undertaker. For sure now, no matter whom he might turn out to be, we'll give him a proper Christian burial. After all the local captains have had a good look at him," said the Garda, "we'll lay him to rest in our own churchyard. Unless someone can identify the body and give him a name."

"That is most kind," remarked Sarah, thinking how others would have planted the unknown stranger in any plot of ground. It was charitable of the town to bury the stranger on holy ground. Some pressure must have been placed upon the church to accept the unusual burial.

"'Tis the least we can do for the poor fellow," agreed the official.

"Do you think you can take me to him now, Constable?" asked Robert.

"Aye, if you are willing to, sir. I'll bring you there myself. 'Tis my own brother-in-law's undertaking business in which we have laid him out in. Not far from the harbor, it is. Will you be after following me over there?"

"Aye," agreed Robert with a sharp, efficient nod, placing his hat on his head in preparation to leave. He turned to the second mate.

"Mr. Litton, I'd like you take command while I'm gone. Have the hands finish the duties that were set for today. And I shall need you to take over my navigational lesson with the midshipmen at midday."

"Aye, aye, sir." The second mate nodded, tipping his hat.

He gave Robert a questioning glance at her. What was to be done about her?

"I'm going with you, Lieutenant," she said firmly.

"It'll be no fit place for a lady," protested the constable. "You might take to fainting, ma'am. And I carry no smelling salts upon my person."

"The body will be quite spoiled," agreed Robert. "I imagine a most unpleasant sight and odor awaits us. The corpse has undoubtedly been battered about the sea for the last few days. No doubt it will be in a dreadful state for viewing by anyone, Mistress Duncan."

"I've seen dead bodies before," she said, remaining firm in her resolve to go. She looked Robert directly in the eye, reminding him that as a wise woman, she had already been a witness to the grim reaper's handiwork. She was not afraid.

A light of admiration shone in his eyes at her fortitude. She truly had a brave, stubborn spirit. He nodded in agreement.

"You shall join us, if that be your desire, ma'am. We depart immediately."

Chapter 7

They were conveyed in the village constable's black carriage to the undertaker's place of business. It was located on the edge of the harbor village. In a whitewashed stone cottage located off the main road, the body of the deceased had been laid out in the undertaker's public viewing room.

Most of the villagers had already taken a look at the unknown deceased. Some of the locals, mostly married women, lit candles in St. Mary's Church afterwards. They gave thanks to all the saints that they did not know him. Many had been afraid that the dead man might be their husband or one of their sons, who were out at sea. None as yet, had been able to give the deceased a name.

The fact the deceased had been murdered brought a dark air of gloom over the village. Old rivalries and hostile grudges were openly reviewed. Some bitter arguments were relived in the market place. The village was tense with suspicion. They wondered what evil had been dropped on their doorstep. The quicker the murdered man was identified and buried, the better.

Sarah held up a rose-scented handkerchief over her nose. She mentally braced herself before entering the room.

While it was true she had been in the presence of the dead before, it was also a fact that this was the first time she had seen one which had ripened over several days. Not to mention battered by the sea almost beyond recognition.

The horrible stench hit her all at once as she stood at the parlor door. It was worse than the smell in the ship's hull. Involuntary, she stepped back.

Get a hold of yourself! 'Tis naught but a poor, dead soul awaiting you in there. You've seen such before.

Robert put a firm, steadying hand beneath her elbow.

"You don't have to go through with this," he said in a soft voice, whispering in her ear. "I will not think any less of you if you should desire to wait outside in the carriage instead. This will be most unpleasant."

"I'm after making for another try," she said firmly, steeling herself once more, better prepared. She told herself she would look the body over as if it were merely a type of study examination created by her mother.

Gladys had always kept her by her side when examining patients. As early as the tender age of six, she'd been taught what signs of illness to look for in the sick, learning the methods to cure and ease pain.

Now she was once more the pupil, examining, thinking of the various ways which might have caused the dead man's demise. How had this all come about? How had he been murdered at sea? And more importantly, who did it and why?

This particular examination was to be unlike any tutoring she had ever had. She had never viewed a murdered man's corpse. But she wanted to try and understand the events leading up to his untimely death.

Could it be that the assassin who'd tried to poison the Captain had been involved in this crime, as well? Or was it simply a coincidence tying them together by time, she wondered?

She quickly glanced at Robert to view his reaction.

He had straightened himself in alert readiness. It was evident he was preparing himself for the worst. She could not help but ponder if the dead man had been one of The Brunswick's missing crewmembers? If so, which one? Could he be the drowned steward or the runaway deserter? In a moment they would know for certain.

Robert stood behind her. He held her shoulders firmly with his strong hands. He was ready to prop her up, if necessary.

She was very aware of his touch. It was a comforting sensation, feeling his fingers supporting her. She knew she would not faint because of it.

Candles were lit about the room for the viewing. It was a thoughtful gesture and she was touched by the consideration of the villagers. They had given the unknown man the same respect as they would have one of their own.

A flat table performed as a bed. It was covered in white linen. The edges of three linens hung over the sides, draping the corpse. The unknown man was completely covered. Only the very crown of the deceased's head, clean-shaven by the women of the village, was bare. His body was facing the foot of the made up bed, as was the custom.

It was believed that by placing the dead in this manner, it might avert the misfortune of being cursed by the deceased's living spirit. And as the man had been murdered, they did not wish to have his ghost linger.

Her first impression was that this was not a very large man. He appeared to be about her height, and therefore not very tall. It might be Jeremy Kaye, she decided, not having a description of the steward, John Stafford. But she remembered that the young seaman had been only slightly taller than herself.

And Robert, how would he feel if it did turn out to be Jeremy? Would he be relieved because he no longer had the responsibility of capturing the deserter, possibly having him placed in prison? Or would he feel guilty because the lad had drowned trying to reach shore after he jumped ship?

Glancing over at his grim profile, it was difficult to tell.

* * *

In a corner of the viewing room sat an old woman dressed all in black, a comfy, long wool shawl wrapped about her. She was keeping vigil near the body. The old mourner had been tranquilly making lace by an open window until they entered the room.

Upon seeing them, she began to conspicuously start wailing and weeping.

"Musha, musha, the poor, poor man," moaned aloud the mourner in Irish. The mourner looked at Sarah. "He was such a good soul, so full o' life was he when he lived. Such an excellent provider, so kind hearted t' his fellow men, he was. The poor, poor sod."

She paused to look them over carefully, her eyes assessing them.

It was evident the village had thought of everything, even to hire a professional mourner. For who knew if the dead man found in the sea might not be one of their own?

The old woman eyed Robert's naval uniform and added clearly in English, "And such an excellent sailor was he. So good at his duties was he, aye. To think he died loyally serving his king and country. 'Tis terrible! Oh, woe . . ."

She beat her chest with a small, clenched fist, grasping a large wood cross that hung from her ample bosom. Dramatically, she held the religious symbol up to the light of the window, making the devout sign of the cross.

"Such an excellent father and provider was the good man. Good Lord, show mercy on his pitiful, sin-filled soul!"

The professional mourner heaved a large sigh of woe and bent her head completely downward in a final show of sorrow.

Overtaken by grief for the unknown seaman, she fell heavily against the sturdy wood chair, apparently overcome by her own mournful sobbing. It appeared she had collapsed.

Sarah moved towards the old woman to check and see if she needed aid. She was about to touch her when suddenly the self-same lady brusquely held out her hand. It appeared from under the long, enveloping black shawl.

"Uh, hmm," murmured the mourner, clearing her throat. She rubbed her pale thin fingers against her thumb in the universal gesture for blunt. A tip was expected.

"Right," replied Robert, automatically removing a guinea from his coat pocket. He put it into the mourner's outstretched hand.

The mourner bit into the coin.

Nodding, she smiled and said, "Long life t' ye, Commander . . . and may I never attend your funeral." The performance had come to an end. She quietly returned to her lace making.

The moment had come to stand closer to the man, to see who it was. Sarah felt Robert's sturdy fingers dig into her shoulders.

The Garda pulled back the white linen.

"It's our missing steward, John Stafford," he said quietly.

He had immediately recognized the knitted tunic. The dark blue woolen still held the unique pattern of the steward's cable knitted garment. The dead man's body was battered. His eyes were missing. The fish had already made food of him.

"John always wore that particular pattern. See the double row of circles knit there." He pointed to a part of the ruined tunic that had remained intact by the shoulder.

The close-knit circles of the tunic were called "beehives" by island knitters. The pattern was so-called because they resembled a bee's honeycomb when knitted together in a cluster. The torn garment was shredded, but a good portion of the sturdy wool threads had held together.

"Those two rows are followed by a straight knit cable row, which was typical of the ones Captain Jackson's servant wore. I have seen that small, gold cross he wears about the neck on Stafford many a time at meals. It always fell out of his shirt and caught the candlelight when he bent to serve the side dishes."

He seemed lost in thought for a moment, remembering the living presence of the dead man. "Aye, it is him, John Stafford."

The Garda gave him a questioning look, wanting to learn more about the dead man.

"And who was this John Stafford? Was he a member of your crew, Commander?"

Robert nodded. "He was . . . Stafford was Captain Jackson's servant whom we thought had been tossed overboard by a wave and drowned."

"So you knew him well, sir?"

"Aye." He nodded and proceeded to explain how it had come about that the steward had gone missing during the tempest.

The constable picked up a white cloth in which was wrapped a weapon, a sharp knife. He showed it to him. The blade, stained by the blood of the dead man, glinted in the sunlight.

"Do you have any idea, as to who might have stabbed him? It was found in his back. 'Tis thought to be the true cause of his death."

"Regrettably, none," he replied, shaking his head.

He glanced at Sarah. All the color had drained from her face. She tensed, leaning against him for support.

She stared at the dead man and shook uncontrollably. She was frightened out of her wits.

"What is it?" he asked

"'Tis h-him. The ghost!" she said, swallowing down her fear. She turned around to face him. Her blue eyes were wide with astonished shock.

The dead man lying before her was none other than the supposedly fake poltergeist she had encountered in the hull. He was the ghostly vision who had greeted her and Jeremy. The same dead seaman who had pointed an accusing finger at them. But now he was no longer entangled in seaweed. He was no longer a prankster's idea of a joke. He was very real.

* * *

They agreed that nothing would be said to the crew about Sarah having recognized the dead man. The constable of the port agreed with Robert's decision, as well. If the knowledge that a murdered man's spirit had been seen wandering about the English frigate, it could cause a mass desertion of both The Brunswick and the harbor.

As it was, several members of the crew were already on edge because of Captain Jackson's death. They wondered if a plague might strike them all down. Who was next?

Robert paid off the old mourner with one gold guinea to keep her silent. She had nodded her gray head and agreed to do as asked. Worriedly, they left the undertaker's house.

"It would worsen matters if it were made known that the steward's spirit had made an appearance in the hull shortly after he'd been murdered," he said as the carriage carried them back to the harbor. "The Brunswick would be labeled a cursed coffin ship. The men would refuse to continue serving if they thought that she might carry them to their grave. Aye, some might even take it into their feeble heads to do as Jeremy did and jump ship."

Sarah quietly listened. She ran her hands nervously over the lace of her gown. She had not recovered from the viewing of the corpse.

She knew he was right in his assumptions about his men. Seamen were notoriously superstitious. They who made their living on the precarious seas looked to nature to give them a sign about their future. Strange beliefs and folklore sprung up as a result.

Sometimes she had watched helplessly as frightened sailors and fishermen labeled the most defenseless person or animal as a 'Jonah.' They blamed the hapless creature for putting the ill wind of fortune that sometimes blew their way upon them.

She had herself faced time and again these superstitious beliefs. Once she witnessed firsthand the cruelty caused by such a dark assumption. A fisherman discouraged by days of poor catch and foul weather, blamed his black cat.

The animal was venomously accused by its master as cursed. He blamed the poor creature for all his troubles. Every error was laid at the animal's feet.

She watched as the fisherman viciously threw the wretched animal into the harbor. The cat meowed piteously to be rescued. Paddling its paws to keep afloat, the animal kept its head barely above water.

The man rowed away without a backward glance.

Feeling pity for the creature's plight, Sarah grabbed a poled fishing net and scooped it out of the cold sea. Wrapping the wet animal in her comfy shawl, she put it in her own boat and took it home. She named it in Irish, Lucky, *Amharach*. It lived out peacefully the remainder of its days on her mother's island home.

Sagely, she nodded in agreement to his suggestion not to say anything.

Aye, the lieutenant is right. I had best be quiet for now about what had transpired in The Brunswick's hull between Jeremy and the dead man's ghost. It would not do the living aboard any good to know what occurred.

"What shall we do next?" she asked. "Do you think that Jeremy's disappearance is connected with Stafford's death? It is almost certain the lad played some part in the murder of the captain's steward. Did not the ghost point its white fingers accusingly at him? And didn't Jeremy jump ship the following day? Perhaps he was afraid to be caught?"

She shivered. Seeing the apparition's earthly body had unnerved her.

"I am as certain as you that Jeremy was somehow tied to the steward's death," he said. "But what if he was only one of several men involved? What if there remains another murderer aboard? Perhaps other mutineers are quietly planning another act of infamy to spring upon us?"

He shook his head.

"Nay, Mistress Duncan, we are far from finished with this mystery and even further from understanding why this path of destruction was chosen. We have much to learn once we are back aboard. It is now my turn to ask the questions."

Chapter 8

Upon returning to the ship Robert began to make inquiries as to whom Jeremy had been spending his off-duty time with. As he had surmised before, the lad was not well liked, very few of the hands had been on sociable terms with the sneering topsails man.

"He was a queer lad, Commander," said one of Jeremy's berth mates, the old toothless ship's cook. "Aye, right shy he was . . . about certain things, sir."

"Such as?"

The old man scratched his balding head and grinned. A devilish smile lit his face.

"He wouldn't be caught with his knickers down. When we took our monthly baths, he'd shy off by himself. He wouldn't let any of us come near him. Must've thought he would catch his death if he left them breeches of his off. Aye, sir, sometimes it made me wonder what he had hidden beneath them layers. Do ye think he had some gold hid on him, sir? Was that why he jumped ship? He didn't want anyone else to know and steal it from him, sir?"

"I rather doubt it, Baker," he replied, with a small smile.

He knew many sailors were on the look-out for hidden treasure, the mythic Aladdin's cave. Indeed some seamen enlisted hoping to make a quick fortune off of captured enemy cargo and warships.

The truth was that such bounty brought an ordinary

seaman little reward. Although recruitment advertisers played up the myth of immense plunder. Usually, the monetary awards received for the capture of a warship went directly into the captain's pockets and the highest ranking officers. The rest of the crew saw very little of the prize money.

"Most likely the lad suffered from some contagion that he did not wish t' have bandied about. And being modest, he hid it out of some sense of shame."

"But, sir, most of us aboard suffer from one kind of condition or 'nother," said the cook, not understanding how the young seaman could hide such a thing from his fellow shipmates. But then Jeremy had always been rather odd.

"Ye know, sir, the lad told us he was an orphan. He said that he was completely alone in the world . . . aye, that one never trusted his secrets to any of us. More silent than a mummer was he about his past. He wouldn't share any tales about his life before he came aboard, sir. A strange one that lad was. He never quite fit with the rest of us, Commander."

"Did he keep a knife about his person, do you know?" asked Robert, changing the subject, thinking of the corpse lying in the undertaker's parlor in Dingle.

"Aye, a penknife he used to whittle with, sir. Once I caught him practice throwing it at a piece of wood. It was late one night during the second dog watch. I warned him to keep the knife safely hid away in his kit."

"Did perchance this blade have a whale bone handle?" he asked sharply.

"Aye, it did, Lieutenant. I do remember that the captain's steward came from below deck and when he saw Jeremy with it, he lit into the lad. He told him he'd take it and have the point broke off by the gunner's hammer on the hatch band seeing how Captain Jackson liked his ship sweet and clean. Not full of blood baths between shipmates like ye have on some of them other vessels. Aye, Stafford was fair afraid that the lad might hurt somebody with it, sir."

Robert nodded. So the knife had led them back to the dead steward and whatever his relationship with Jeremy might have been. But had the two men been friends or foes? It was difficult to know now that one was missing, and the other dead.

"Anything else ye be wanting t' know, Commander?" asked the cook. It was nearing midday and he had yet to prepare the crew's mess.

"Aye, I've just one more question. Before then, did Jeremy and John Stafford ever quarrel or disagree on anything?"

"Nay, not that I know of, sir," answered the cook, shaking his gray head. "There is something ye might be interested in, though . . ."

The cook hesitated, looking around to see if they were being observed.

His long, gray beard almost touched Robert as he leaned closer. His breath smelled strongly of tobacco and rum. A fact the commander chose to ignore. He needed the man's loyalty and information more than a clean breath.

"Jeremy left his ditty behind, sir. He didn't take it with him when he abandoned ship. It be still aboard with the rest of the crew's. I saw it myself this morning, as I pulled me own kit out for a shave."

"Thank you, Mr. Baker. You may return to your duties," Robert said, dismissing the man with a nod.

The cook pulled on his forelock in respect and stepped back into the galley. The young commander turned and walked towards the hatch leading to the lower decks. He had come no closer to discovering the truth.

The evidence concerning the steward's death lay directly connected with a seaman everyone aboard unanimously labeled as being peculiar. Jeremy had been a young seaman far from home who had managed to alienate himself from his shipmates.

It was more than odd. It begged the question, why had the lad taken to the sea in the first place? Was he running away from something unsavory back home?

Perhaps Jeremy's ditty bag might tell him more. Perhaps there were letters and other revealing personal paraphernalia in it. Aye, it might tell him more about the missing seaman. He would have to take a look.

He descended to the middle deck in search of the deserter's ditty. What Baker had told him was true. Jeremy had not taken it with him. The canvas bag, which contained all the possessions of importance to a seaman, was in a pile where the noncommissioned crew kept their belongings. He removed the bag from the pile and brought it to his cabin.

Sarah, who had been taking a nap, sat up. She had been reading one of his books on his berth when she fell asleep. Her reading had become a pleasurable habit. It was one she had taken up since coming aboard. To Robert's delight he was able to discuss some of his favorite topics with her.

Nodding to her pleasantly, he greeted her. "I hope I haven't disturbed your slumber, Mistress Duncan."

"Ye needn't worry, Lieutenant," she replied, curious as to why he had decided to visit her at midday. Usually, well occupied by his duties, he did not approach her for idle conversation at this time.

Aye, she thought observing him. There was always a purpose behind what he did.

"It is glad I am that you woke me," she said. "I promised Mr. Baker I'd give him some of my rosemary oil to use in tonight's meal. So what brings ye here? Normally, I do not have the pleasure of your company until evening mess."

He gently closed the cabin door behind him.

"I have need of some privacy and this was the only place I could think of where none of my crew would observe me," he explained, emptying the contents of the canvas ditty onto the small writing table set against the cabin wall.

Before him were the usual items one would expect a sailor to carry, a small handmade mirror set into a wood holder, a brass traveling quill pen, an ink container, a few sheets of paper, a sewing kit with buttons, a deck of cards, a pocket Bible, a wood comb, a tin cup, and eating utensils. An eating knife of some sort usually would be included along with a shaving kit—both were missing from the ditty.

He took the Bible and looked inside. He hoped to find further information. Happily, he was not disappointed. The front page provided some information on the Bible's original owner.

Turning a page, he read aloud the words written on the inside.

"If found return to Mrs. Jemima Kaye, North Port Street, Portsmouth, England. Most interesting." he said, looking at the neat slanted handwriting. "Now, that is intriguing."

"Why?" she asked, peeking over his shoulder to look at the writing.

"Because Jeremy enlisted as a bachelor," he replied. "Whoever this Mrs. Kaye is, Jeremy must not have given her much thought."

"And you conclude this because he did not enlist as a married man?" she asked.

"Aye, that and because he never wrote or mentioned her to his shipmates." He scratched his chin thoughtfully. "He never mentioned her to any of the hands."

"He may have decided to keep their relationship a secret."

Robert shook his head.

"If he had died at sea, she would have deserved the right to a widow's pension. But this way, keeping her hid from the ship's list, meant she would not receive a single sixpence of recompense from the Royal Admiralty."

"Could it be that this lady is not his spouse? Could she be perhaps his mother or sister-in-law? Maybe she is his brother's wife?"

"Aye, that's possible . . . but again, why did he not make mention of her to the rest of the men and list her as his surviving kin? Why did he tell all and sundry that he was an orphan, without any relations? Prodigiously intriguing, don't you think?"

"Perhaps they quarreled and he no longer wished to have his name associated with hers?" she suggested.

"But to alienate her from him to the point where he did not want his name connected to hers even upon death? That seems rather cruel," he said, rubbing the back of his neck in frustration. "None of this makes sense."

Eyeing the address, she asked, "How soon will we be voyaging on to Portsmouth?"

"In about one day's time. The repairs are almost finished. I can no longer delay our return without receiving a censoring reprimand from the Admiralty for its tardiness. Regrettably, there will be no time to return to Varrik Island to check on your mother and Captain Jackson. But if you wish, I could send out one of my officers to see how they are faring before we voyage on south to England."

"Nay, there is no need. I know that my godfather, Duncan, will seek me out if there be any further news from my mother," she said. She thought warmly of the old fisherman who was her godfather.

"He is the one I told you who rescued me from the

[115]

sea as a baby. He has always watched over us. And if Captain Jackson were doing worse, Mother would have sent us word. No, 'tis time we went on to Portsmouth and found this Mrs. Kaye. Perhaps she will be the one who will be able to tell us something more about Jeremy and his association with the captain's steward."

"You are resolved to resume this search?" he asked, wondering if the charade of pretending to be his betrothed had become too much of a burden.

The dangers surrounding them, the captain's poisoning and the steward's murder, made clear the real perils facing anyone associated with The Brunswick. She might not want to remain with him.

"Perhaps you should return to the safety of your mother's island home before you find yourself badly hurt or injured," he said, frowning as he eyed her delicate features.

He continued, "With a madman on the loose, set upon murdering various members of the crew, regardless of rank, who knows what might happen to you. You are an easy target, vulnerable to attack."

She looked up at him. She wasn't willing to abandon the search. This murderer needed to be stopped. And she was willing to help as much as she was able. Nay, she didn't want to quit. Although he didn't want to say it, she knew he needed her help.

"I can face all the perils you fear. I'm ready to continue on, Lieutenant Smythe. I want to remain aboard with you," she said stoutly.

Robert could not explain it, but a sharp pang of relief hit the region of his heart. The protective feelings he had begun to have for her, he did not wish to examine. But the truth was he had begun to grow fond of the wise woman. In the short time she had been aboard, he had become accustomed to having her with him.

He enjoyed their times alone together. Sarah had a lively wit. When they played cards, she made an excellent partner. She was an amiable companion.

He noted with a feeling akin to jealousy that several of the other bachelors aboard, as well as a few of the married officers, were equally captivated by her. He did not blame them. How could he?

The way she cheerfully pitched in to give a hand to everyone, from the cook to the officers' wives, had earned the respect of the entire crew. It was truly admirable. She may not have been born a titled lady, but she behaved like one.

"I feel myself to be a veritable cad, keeping you involved in this sordid business," he confessed. "I ought to order you home, to return you to the safekeeping of your mother. It's wrong of me to continue to keep you. It's evident I am putting you at peril, risking your life as I blindly pursue a dangerous villain."

"No," she said softly. "I want to find this madman as much as you do. If it is Jeremy, then let us track him down together and discover why he felt compelled to do this. Nay, it would be wrong of me to leave."

She looked at him, her own feelings about leaving him barely hid in her eyes. She had no desire to go home. She wanted to remain with him.

This seaman was one of the most fascinating men she had ever met. Intelligent and attractive, he had proven himself to be both a gentleman and a worthy friend. She now desperately wanted to bring to light all the mystery surrounding the ill fortune concerning the murder and Captain Jackson's poisoning. She owed it to him and the dead steward.

He mustn't send me away—he mustn't, she thought silently, willing him to permit her to stay by his side. She knew, however, better than to argue.

If Lieutenant Smythe decided she was not to remain a minute longer on board the vessel, the hands would obediently carry out his command and she would be, if necessary, forcibly removed. He could send her packing with a mere nod.

Aye, there was no use in arguing, she despaired. But that didn't mean she couldn't try and persuade him to let her remain.

"I am as much entangled in the murder of the captain's steward and all that surrounds it, as you are," she said, continuing to persuade him.

Her eyes silently pleaded with him to let her stay.

Had she not proven herself? She had handled life aboard the small frigate with great aplomb. By tending the ill and hurt had she not proven herself to be an asset? Silently, her blue cornflower eyes pleaded with him.

"Aye, well then . . . you may stay," he relented.

Impulsively, joyous over his decision, she threw her arms around his neck. Her lips parted as she looked up at him, tilting her head invitingly as they gazed into each other's eyes. Bending his head, he responded by kissing her, his arms reaching around her waist, drawing her closer to him as their mouths met. Her lips tingled deliciously, her blood sang with pleasure as she tightened her hold on him.

Heart pounding, he abruptly pulled her out of his arms, before he completely lost control. She was so damnably beautiful.

"Forgive me," he said, breathing heavily, angry with himself. "That was unforgiveable. I shouldn't have done that."

Puzzled by his reaction, she asked, "Why?"

Was kissing her so disagreeable?

He saw the look of hurt in her eyes. He reached out to touch her, to draw her back into his arms . . . and then caught himself. He wanted to kiss her again, but his conscience dictated his actions. Ah, damn but he wanted her. If he were being honest with himself, he would admit that he'd wanted her from the moment he met her. She completely captivated him in every way. *Damn. Damn. Damn.*

Deliberately, he stepped away from her.

He had no right to touch her. She was not his. She was here doing him a favor, he reminded himself. God help him if anything should happen to her. He would never be able to forgive himself if one single hair on her beautiful, golden head should be harmed.

He glanced over at the weapon that that been used to kill Stafford, lying next to Jeremy's Bible. Dark, blood stains remained on the blade. He strengthened his resolve to go forward with their search, while reaffirming his need to protect this courageous and unique woman.

"I have a duty to perform," he said stiffly, as if that was all the explanation that he needed to give her for his behavior. "We shall head on to Portsmouth and see if we can unravel this tangled mystery involving a frightening ghost, a runaway lad, and a villainous murderer."

She nodded, understanding. Duty came first. Although hurt by his rejection, she knew better than to question his actions. He was the one in command and she had to obey. Her gaze turned back to the map he was pointing at.

He drew a line from Ireland down to Port Sea Island. There on the southern part of England, the naval harbor of Portsmouth was located. They were to travel there on the morrow.

* * *

That evening as Robert played the mandolin for her, she felt restless, knowing that the next day they would be entering English waters. She was excited that they'd soon be uncovering the mysterious relationship between the runaway seaman and Jemima Kaye, but what occupied her thoughts the most was Robert. She smiled as she usually did, watching him play, but she couldn't stop thinking about how he'd held back from kissing her earlier that day.

She'd sensed the moment he'd withdrawn from her that he'd purposefully held back, behaving nobly, stopping himself from becoming physically intimate with her. But did she want him to do that, to continue to hold back?

Shaking her head, she felt a mounting frustration growing inside her. She desired him. She wanted him to touch her in the intimate manner a man did when he was attracted to a woman. She acknowledged to herself, she craved his touch. She'd enjoyed the feel of his hands on her body. What would it be like if he'd made love to her? She glanced surreptitiously at Robert as he plucked the strings of the mandolin, wondering how those same fingers would feel brushing along her skin. She blushed at her own thoughts.

When she had been betrothed to John, she had given herself to him, knowing that they were to marry, and yearning to experience that special loving that men and women have experienced since time began. Was it wrong for her to want that again? Robert was not her betrothed, so was she behaving like one of those mistresses or dockside strumpets? Nay, she was not. That was not her way. Oh, she had always been a lively and friendly woman, but she had never behaved in an improper manner. She was a wise woman and her work was of an intimate nature, so she had always been careful of her behavior.

What of the memory of her fiancé? Was it wrong for her to want another man's arms around her? She had loved John, and had greatly cared for him. She had wanted to marry him. And after he died, she had mourned his death. But as a healer she had always understood the fleeting nature of life. Illness and accidents, and yes, the evil of others, could deal a cruel blow. The time they had together could be snuffed out in a moment, so was it wrong for her to want some happiness while it was here in front of her? Sarah recalled the encouraging words of John's mother—to continue on with her life—to let herself love again . . . and she realized she was ready to move on, ready to love, and she hoped that Robert would be that man.

She began to sway to the music, letting it envelope her, letting the tension from discovering the identity of the ghost and the murder weapon drop away as she sipped her dinner wine. She leaned against him in a companionable manner as he played the instrument, enjoying the music.

Maybe it was the cozy atmosphere they'd created in the cabin with the music and candlelight, maybe it was because she didn't care about propriety anymore, maybe she was drunk on wine and whimsy, but she knew, without a doubt that she wanted him. Her feelings for him had grown since she beheld him on her doorstep, with his captain slung over his shoulders. What a strong and brave man he was. She admired him greatly, but as a woman, she could not help but be attracted to him. He was just so beautiful.

She laid her head against his shoulder and without a thought, as if second nature took control of her movements, she reached for his hand and brought it to her face.

He stopped his strumming, and putting down the instrument, he turned fully to her and began to run his thumb back and forth over her lips. She closed her eyes and sighed.

"Sarah, you are the loveliest woman I have ever beheld." he said in a husky voice, looking into her bright blue eyes. "It's been a long time since I've lain with a woman. If I stay here much longer, I won't—that is—I want—"

"Shhh . . . ," she whispered, placing her fingers on his lips to hush him. "Robert, I've not been with a man since my fiancé died . . . I cared deeply for him, and I was true and loyal to him, but enough time has passed now, for me to . . ." She blushed and took a deep breath, wondering if he would think her too bold, but she didn't care, because she needed him. Right now, she needed his touch more than anything. She smiled and caressed his face. "Robert, I want you too . . . please, make love to me."

His breath caught at the look in her eyes. He nodded, wrapping his arms around her, lowering his head, gently kissing her. She felt her blood begin to warm as his tongue opened her mouth. Responding, she opened her own, their lips and tongues meeting, entwining, while her heart pounded in anticipation.

She wanted him. She realized that she'd desired him since the first moment she set eyes on his half-clad body in the sweat hut. She'd never beheld such a handsome and sensual man.

Placing her hands on his naval whites, she began unbuttoning the gold buttons on the front flap of his breeches. Pulling the fabric down, she cradled his manhood, gently stroking him, enjoying the feel of the soft skin, while rubbing her fingers along the hard shaft, encouraging it to grow.

He threw his head back and uttered a soft groan. "Sarah . . . I'm completely under your spell. You've bewitched me."

His hands moved over her body in turn, stroking her back, running up the sides of her ribcage and around to the back of her bodice. Unlacing it, he pulled the garment away from her body. She now breathed freely as his hands reached out to cup her breasts, his dark brown eyes shining with admiration.

Bending his head, he sought out her nipples with his mouth, sucking on each in turn, playfully flicking his tongue back and forth around the dark center of the globes until they stood erect. A blooming desire overtook her as a warm, pulsing in her lower region made her crave more.

She unbuttoned her skirt and with his help pulled it and her undergarments off, tossing them aside. She shivered in the cool night air, wrapping her arms around herself, standing before him in her garters and stockings, the only covering she wore. Although, she was no longer a shy virgin, she still felt nervous. She hadn't lain with a man in a long time and she wanted to please Robert so very much.

"My God, you are breathtaking," he said in a raspy voice. He looked hungrily at her exposed body in the candlelight, in awe of her beauty.

He got down on his knees in front of her, and placed his hands on her waist, drawing her close. He wrapped his arms around her and pressed his head against her belly.

"Breathe, my sweet," he said in a soothing voice.

She hadn't realized she was holding her breath. She let it out with a gasp and grasped his shoulders.

"So much—I want you so much," he whispered.

He looked up at her then, his eyes full of passion and something else too—reverence. He reached out and undid the garters holding the stockings up. Slowly, savoring the undressing, he rolled each one down, placing a trail of kisses on her bared skin as he did so until she was completely naked.

Drawing her close to him, he opened the lips of her moist center with his fingers and began to massage her there, in lazy circles. Then he moved closer and touched her with his tongue, tasting her, teasing her, making her gasp and moan, making her throb with unbearable pleasure. Pulling back, he stood up and removed his breeches, then swung her up in his arms and turning, laid her on the bed.

Beverly Adam

He gazed down at her, losing himself once more in the beauty of her eyes. He wanted her to be sure. "Are you certain?"

Nodding, she reached up, pulled his head down, and kissed him fervently. He moaned and kissed her back, their tongues playing and dancing. His fingers reached down between her legs once more and entered her, playing her as he'd played the mandolin earlier. Such clever fingers, she thought. And then she could think no more as he built the pressure up inside her to a bursting crescendo.

"Robert!"

"Yes, my sweet?" he asked with a roguish grin, as he continued to finger her slick folds.

"Please, come inside me!"

He was nothing if not compliant to her wishes in this regard. She grabbed his shoulders as he positioned himself between her legs. Lifting her bottom up, he thrust into her and groaned with the pleasure of it—the magnificent, hot pleasure of being inside Sarah.

The burst of pleasure she'd felt when he was using his fingers on her was nothing compared to this feeling building inside of her now. In tune to a beautiful rhythm, they moved together, faster and faster until she could no longer stop the tide of feeling washing over her. She cried out in wonder, as he pumped in and out a few more times, before pulling out with a shout and letting his seed spill out onto the bed.

Lying back with a heavy breath, he held her in his arms, stroking her hair and back, and confessed, "It was as I'd dreamed it would be between us . . . I will never forget the gift you've given me tonight."

"Nor, I," she said with a smile in her voice.

He kissed her once more, dreamily, lazily, and brushed his fingers through her hair. Comforted by his touch and reassuring words, she smiled and fell into a deep sleep.

In the morning, when she awoke, he was gone. He'd returned to his duties as commander of the ship. She knew better than to disturb him. When they reached England, everything between them would change. She knew it. She would return to her life as an Irish healer and Robert to his duties as an English naval captain, and they would part.

Last night had been magical. Robert had called their joining "a gift," and she told herself that was how she was going to think of it, as well. She would not attach any strings to it. She was not going to ruin their friendship by making any demands. It would be wrong to do so. He had a commitment and a duty to his career. And she—she had her calling.

"Don't expect anything more from him than that . . . be happy you had last night," she told herself. And although her heart ached at the thought of their eventual parting, she knew it was for the best.

Chapter 9

In the early morning, The Brunswick arrived in English waters. The frigate tranquilly tied up without incidence in the Naval Dockyard at Port Sea, its home berth in Portsmouth. It had passed the Mill Pond, an inlet from the sea, while entering the harbor during the last moments of waning sunlight. Golden rays bounced off the water's reflection around the small ship as its hands tied her ropes.

Larger first-rated ships of the line with their three decks and eighty-some odd guns were anchored farther out at sea. These bulky ships of the line rarely entered the narrow harbor, which the much smaller Brunswick had easily passed.

Off in the close distance from Portsmouth, was the Isle of Wight. It protected the harbor from the English Channel. Ships of the Royal Navy were moored in the stretch of water in between, called the Spithead, awaiting orders.

Unbeknownst to the master and commander of The Brunswick, the crew had planned an engagement party for that evening for him and his lovely betrothed. Mistress O' Grady, the master gunner's wife, had taken it upon herself personally to see to it that the lady was kept well occupied with sewing and mending all day.

So busy was she kept that Sarah didn't have time to notice the decorations and preparations that the officers and hands were planning. Flower rosettes made from dyed blue gunny sacks were swaged along the ship's polished rails. Paper lights were strung from wood poles to be lit as fairy lanterns at night on the top deck.

One of the younger petty officers kept her away from the cook's galley, a place she often visited to offer her assistance throughout the day.

"Mr. Baker is in one of his unpredictable moods, ma'am," said the young officer with his fingers crossed behind his back in a lie. "He told me himself that he needed to be left in peace. In confidentiality, I must tell you he's working on a new recipe and wants to surprise you with it himself, ma'am. It would be best if you stayed away from the galley today. He wants to try out some of the fancy herbs you've been giving him to season the food with, ma'am."

So pleased was she that the cook wanted to surprise her with a new recipe using her herbs, she readily agreed not to disturb him. One of the unexpected friendships she had made aboard was with the frigate's taciturn cook. By offering different savory herbs and potent tasting oils from her well-stocked sea chest, she had broken through the cook's usual reserve.

A congenial rivalry had sprung up between the two as to who could find the most interesting spices to season the usual bland offerings. As a result of their joint efforts, the meals served from the galley had greatly improved, to the general delight of everyone aboard.

The young petty officer had spoken a half-truth. They were pulling out all the stops for supper. The cook intended on providing some savory surprises. What few remaining animals left from the officer's pen were about to be put to good use for this special meal.

On the menu there was to be the usual first course of vegetable soup with boiled potatoes, followed by the second course consisting of spitted venison with parsley herbs and carrots with caramelized onions swimming in cream, a delicacy the seamen had not enjoyed for several months. It was to be served with several covered side dishes of curried rabbit, ham, and more vegetables, with sweet lemon pudding.

The last course, the dessert, was to be the highlight of the evening's menu. As good fortune should have it, Mr. Baker had a brother who was in fact a superb baker living in Portsmouth Point. The brother had been contacted the day before by a passing fishing vessel on its way to England to prepare for this special event. Not only did the baker know how to bake bread, but had a noted delicate hand with pastry confections.

The baker and his assistants had set about creating the small round cakes known as "maids of honor" and various fruit tarts at his brother's request. In honor of the impending nuptials, he created a superb ginger spiced tea-cake with a sugar-spun replica of The Brunswick perched on top. How the cook had managed such a feat worthy of a high admiral's table was much talked of by all who saw it. For it was truly a lifelike marvel to behold.

The marine fife and drum corps assigned to the frigate would play during the dancing. It would make up the small orchestra for the party.

The hands, delighted to be invited to such a grand affair, sent word to their wives and sweethearts living in Portsmouth and around the neighboring community of Southampton. The ladies were invited to join them for the ball to be given aboard the frigate in honor of their commander and his lovely betrothed.

*　*　*

As the guests began arriving on horseback, foot, and carriage, Sarah appeared on the top deck wearing a blindfold. Earlier that evening Mistress O' Grady had approached her with a request from the commander and the officers.

"They were hoping, Mistress Duncan, as this is to be for many of them their last night aboard, if ye would honor them by wearing your best gown. There's to be a small party before the crew departs for their homes on the morrow."

"Certainly, I would be delighted to," she readily agreed and set about putting on her finest slippers and best gown.

Before she could set foot on the quarter-deck, the master gunner's wife, with a merry twinkle in her eyes, whispered in her ear, "We have a wee bit of a surprise for you and Commander Smythe. This party has been prepared by the entire crew to honor your approaching nuptials."

She froze for a moment, concerned about the extent of their ruse. "Well, then we mustn't disappoint," she said feebly, noting that Robert had joined her.

Feeling a pang of guilt in her stomach, she glanced a little nervously at Robert. She wondered how the members of The Brunswick would react when they later learned the nuptials had been called off. Deceiving these kind people made her feel wretched. She felt unworthy of their kindness. Despite the fact her short-lived deception was a tool for a noble cause, it nonetheless troubled her greatly.

Robert wore his full dress uniform. She couldn't help but admire how handsome he looked. The uniform fit his broad shoulders and cinched his trim waist. His white breeches molded his muscular legs like a second skin. She couldn't help remembering their night together— it was doubly painful to know that they were not, in fact, truly betrothed.

He'd joined her after adjourning an officers' meeting in the wardroom. She'd seen very little of him that day for he'd spent most of it updating the ship's log. He'd held the meeting with the officers in preparation for dismissing the crew and turning the frigate back over to the Royal Admiralty.

He smiled, holding out his white-gloved hand and she took it. She looked at him and wondered what he was thinking. She wondered if he felt as wretchedly as she did.

Mistress O'Grady blindfolded them and then one of the marines opened the door leading out to the deck. It was to be a grand surprise. Their blinds were lifted and Sarah looked out at the lovely preparations.

She felt a lump form in her throat and her eyes filled with tears.

No one had ever honored her in such a touching manner before. The most she could ever hope by way of thanks and recompense from her patients was to be given some livestock, a few goods, and perhaps on rare occasions, a shilling or two, but nothing compared to the delightful celebration that the crew had planned for her and their commander.

"'Tis humbling," she said to Robert as a sea of smiling faces looked up at them standing on the quarter-deck.

"They've been a good crew." He nodded, happy for his men, and proud that The Brunswick had safely docked after spending two years at sea. He looked down at the lovely young woman by his side and experienced a longing he had never allowed himself to feel before. Making love to Sarah had been something he had wanted to do since the moment he set eyes on the golden-haired beauty. He wondered what she was thinking and feeling? Was she regretting their night together or did she wish for more? He sighed and put his thoughts aside for now, but at some point, he would have to speak with Sarah about it.

Suddenly, the crew let out a big cheer. "Hip-Hip-

Huzzah!" Catcalls and whistles of approval quickly followed.

Sarah stood beside him, laughing at the men's good mood. She waved at them and their cheers grew even louder. Aye, she was in high spirits, as well, he thought, as he wrapped his arm around her and drew her closer. He felt some of the tension he'd held since taking over command from Captain Jackson loosen from his shoulders. No great disaster had passed aboard the ship for which the Admiralty could blame him for. The loss of the steward's life had been a tragedy, beyond his control, and therefore he would not be held accountable. The career he'd envisioned for himself at sea in the Royal Navy would continue onward, unchanged. However he did not look forward to informing the steward's sole remaining relative, a spinster of twenty, of her brother's death.

The same, he was certain, would be the judgment concerning the deserter, Jeremy Kaye. That occurrence would be listed by the Royal Admiralty as an act of mutinous treason against king and country. It would have no bearing on how he'd commanded the crew and The Brunswick. It would not reflect poorly upon him.

He knew his men would testify that the lad had been more than treated fairly by him and the other superior ranking officers. No harsh treatment of the young seaman had occurred. There was no reason for Jeremy to have jumped ship.

He frowned as his thoughts turned to darker matters.

The only lingering issue was the matter of the blackguard who tried to kill Captain Jackson. He would not rest until that was resolved. Until then he had to pretend that Captain Jackson had met his maker.

Robert took a tankard from the tray of one of the cabin boys who were serving the crew, and handed Sarah a glass of sherry. Taking a healthy swallow of the brew, he fortified himself for his ongoing investigation into the murder of Captain Jackson. He was thankful he had Sarah's input. Her wisdom and intuition about the nefarious plot was invaluable. But he was concerned for her welfare. For all her experiences as a wise woman, she had led a very sheltered life. And he was worried about putting her in harm's way. Any thoughts of her being hurt caused him to break into a sweat. Nay, he would protect Sarah at all cost. With his very life if he had to. He finished his drink with one final gulp. The spirit was strong, knocking some of the strain out of his weary thoughts of murder and conspiracy.

Grog, the seamen's drink of beer or rum mixed with the usually acrid tasting water supply when at sea, was being liberally passed around. Barrels of fresh brewed beer were rolled up the gang-plank from local taverns to be handed out to the celebrating men.

The hands called for a toast. They stood about on the deck hugging their wives and sweethearts by their sides. Children, dogs, and even a small monkey, joyously ran around chasing each other.

Suddenly, there was silence.

Respectfully quiet, they looked up expectantly at the officers and their commander, with whom they had sailed in fair and foul weather for the past two years. During that time they had taken life saving commands from these superior officers, some of whom were as young as their own sons, working and fighting side-by-side for king and country aboard the frigate.

Lieutenant Litton stepped up to the quarter-deck. He raised his tankard.

"A toast to one of the best first mates I've ever had the privilege to serve under, the man who held us together after Captain Jackson's demise and brought us safely back home . . ." At the mention of Captain Jackson many took their caps off in proper respect for

[132]

the deceased. "Let us toast, ladies and gentlemen, our master and commander, First Lieutenant Smythe and his bonnie bride to-be, Mistress Duncan."

All the men stood out of respect for the couple, their tankards raised.

"I feel certain I am speaking for all of us aboard, Lieutenant Smythe, when we wish you and your lovely lady long life and many years of smooth sailing ahead, sir," said the second in command, raising his tankard in the couple's direction. "To the happy couple!" he toasted and took a hearty swallow of the brew from his own tankard.

The men echoed with hardy cheers of "Hear, Hear, and to Lieutenant Smythe!" All followed the example the lieutenant set, drinking heartily from their tankards.

Robert addressed the crew and their families. "I am a man of few words and so I shall simply say my betrothed and I thank you for your kind thoughts and best wishes."

Unable to resist, he kissed Sarah's hand. He smiled as he watched her cheeks blush becomingly.

Humbled by the kind words of the second mate, he raised his cup in the air and finished by saying, "To the bravest and best crew I've ever had the privilege to serve with. God bless you, gentlemen . . . and God bless the king!"

"To the king!" came back the replay from those below.

It was then that Lieutenant Litton nodded to the marine band orchestra and they began to play. Officers set up into sets for a quadrille led by Robert and Sarah. The crew stood back and watched the handsome commander of The Brunswick and his lovely betrothed as they went through the intricate steps of the dance.

Sarah had danced before at balls held at Brightwood Manor in her home village of Urlingford. She was therefore not afraid to step forth. The quadrille and country dances were familiar to her.

She glided back and forth with little effort on the smooth planks of the top deck in a pair of light-blue dancing slippers. The crossed silver ribbons peeked out from beneath her gown's lace as she twirled under the glittering fairy lights.

Robert, a gleam of admiration in his hazel eyes, took one of her outstretched gloved hands and turned her gently around. She spun gracefully in his guiding arms.

Caught up in the music and the unwavering attraction of seeking out the young commander in the ritual of dance, she barely remembered to switch partners, much to the delight of those watching. All were attentive to the romantic gestures of the handsome couple before them. Many laughed at the face the young woman made as she left the commander's side to dance with her next partner.

When the dance ended, flushed from being the focus of the admiring stares of the handsome officer before her, Sarah finished the quadrille with a gracious curtsey.

The crew applauded the dancers and musicians. The ladies quickly unfolded their silk-covered fans, fluttering them back and forth, giving overheated faces a quick refreshing wave of air. Already many were red-cheeked and merry from the spirits passed around.

The second mate appeared at Robert's side and before she had a moment to straighten, Sarah was claimed for the next dance.

Was it a flight of fancy on her part or did a look of reluctance on the part of Lieutenant Smythe pass across his face as he permitted his second in command to dance with her? Sarah's heart did a little trip at the thought.

Lieutenant Litton noticed his commander's reaction.

"Buck up, Commander," he said cheerfully bowing over her hand. "I just want to dance with your pretty betrothed once. I promise to safely return her to your care when I'm done, sir." But this was not to be . . . as if recognizing a golden opportunity to needle their usually placid first lieutenant, all the superior officers and masters aboard took turns stepping in front of the first mate.

Every time Robert tried to claim her hand for another dance, another seaman stepped in front of him. It was clear a joke was being perpetrated upon the couple. One member of the crew after another presented themselves in front of the increasingly frustrated young commander. Smirking, even the unranked crewmembers intercepted the first mate's advances towards the beautiful Mistress Duncan.

"Sorry, sir," a young gunner barely out of short pants rushed up, "but this is my dance, I believe, sir."

He bowed and whisked her off for a country dance.

"I know you'll be holding her hand for the rest of your life, Lieutenant Smythe, sir. So I thought I best step in and claim one dance now while I can, sir," said a gangly carpenter, taking his chance.

And at the exact moment Robert thought he might have an opportunity to steal a step with her, the brawny master gunner placed himself in line.

Master O'Grady's grin of delight was barely hidden under his tanned face as the Irish giant stepped down upon one of the commander's polished boots, bruising his toes.

"Oh, excuse me, Lieutenant Smythe, sir . . . I did not mean to do ye any harm, sir." The giant shamelessly smiled. "But this being my favorite dance, and the good wife saying how I ought to ask Mistress Duncan whilst she's still aboard, sir . . . well, I thought it best that—"

"That you should dance with my betrothed now while you still have the opportunity," said Robert, finishing the sentence for him with a small sigh.

He had heard the same excuse about thirty times before. He bowed, turning the dance over to the shameless giant, who gently clasped Sarah's small hand in one of his large callused ones. She could not help but smile at him.

The giant bowed to Sarah and over her shoulder gave his wife a knowing wink.

Robert dared a glance in the direction of Mistress O' Grady, the gunner's wife. She openly tittered behind a Japanese painted fan, observing from behind it her husband teasing the good-looking first mate.

Aye, there'd been many a time in the past when this distinguished English officer had broken a lady's heart by not asking her to dance. For sure now to some small extent 'twas grand to see the self-assured Englishman having to experience for once what it felt to be in someone else's less than elegantly polished shoes.

The matron gently patted her bulging front, a sign of the approaching birth of her fifth child. She had experienced two miscarriages and a stillbirth before this one took. Already she had brokered a promise from Sarah to be in attendance at her next birthing. Her two eldest children, ages thirteen and ten, were already serving aboard The Brunswick, learning their trade. The eldest had been recently rated on the ship's books as an able-bodied seaman.

Sarah, during a short breather, asked her if she was nervous about the approaching birth.

"Nay," Mistress O'Grady replied with a proud smile, "I've already given birth between the cannons of this man-of-war. My lads are true sons-of-a-gun, by virtue of having been born aboard The Brunswick. But faith now, it'd be nice for once to have another woman's presence at my next birthing. Aye, I was left quite all on m' own the last time, the men being afraid that I might give birth and up and die."

"Do you have any thoughts as to whether the baby is a boy or girl?"

"That I do . . . I hope this one will be another son. I detest being parted from m' lass. Though thank the heavens above, my youngest sister has seen to it she's got some book learning. Our Mary writes to us often, she does." She added proudly, "'Tis not every seaman's daughter who can brag she can read, ye know. But the letters, though they are a wee bit of comfort to us, are no substitute for having her with us."

She glanced upwards to the riggings above where her two eldest sons sat in the crow's nest, a platform situated at a dizzying height at the top of the mast, observing the party below. The mother nodded to the boys as they waved down at her.

"Aye, it's grand to have me sons hanging about."

It was after Sarah had danced several lively country dances, a sharp pain in her side made her realize she needed to take a rest. With a smile of regret on her face, hugging her side, she turned to the line of gentlemen waiting their turn to dance with her.

"I'm sorry, but I am afraid I've had enough of dancing for tonight. Be assured I'm flattered by your attention, gentlemen. However, I do believe Lieutenant Smythe is about to fetch me some punch and I am going to sit myself down and take a bit of a rest."

Robert, a grin of triumph on his handsome face, held out his arm for her to take. They slowly walked over to the table covered with food and drink. The table was in fact two wide planks that had been laid across guns and covered with a white lace cloth borrowed from one of the hands' wives.

Sarah had witnessed the seamen make use of the long neck barrels of the guns this way many times before when they were eating. There was no room aboard for any real tables. The gunnery instruments were kept at the ready next to the cannons, every bit of space on the fighting vessel being economically used.

[137]

Plate in hand, she began to sample delicacies that the crew of The Brunswick had not had the pleasure to enjoy while at sea. The fresh fruit, diverse vegetable dishes, and unsalted venison were in particular appreciated by the seamen.

For the moment lowly potatoes, beans, dried foods, and limes were overlooked in favor of summer fruits. Fresh peaches, strawberries, apricots, berries, and plums were treated as exotic, succulent delights. And to the men's bored and well-salted taste buds, they were pure ambrosia.

Companionably, Robert stood next to her as they ate.

Barrels, crates, and what few chairs aboard the frigate were placed about the top deck to serve as seats for their guests. The seamen stood gallantly about, letting the ladies and children take what few chairs were available.

The moon shone brightly down upon the frigate as water gently lapped against the hull. One of the marines began to play a romantic sea shanty on his accordion. A member of the crew began to sing, and soon others joined in, and before the next stanza was finished, the entire deck was awash with merry voices.

The seamen unashamedly held their wives and sweethearts, playing peek-a-boo games with the numerous babies sitting on their mothers' laps. Many of the children present were becoming acquainted with their fathers for the first time. Some of the babies had been born while the men were away at sea.

Sarah and Robert sat away from the rest of the party. They looked out over the bulkhead at the romantic moonlit water of the islet in the distance. Their bodies were screened from view of the others. The teasing had ceased. At last they were alone.

She thought back briefly to her first conversation

with the handsome first mate, when he'd told her of his life at sea. She thought it was isolating to be the commander in charge of a naval warship. She'd noticed how he'd had to stand alone—how all the men aboard respected and feared him. And she knew Robert could never be completely open about himself with anyone. She'd discovered that as the commanding first mate, he'd always had to make difficult decisions with an air of certainty, which at times she could tell he was far from feeling.

Aye, she decided, to be always in command must be a lonely duty. It was one, she noticed, he'd not been able to share with another. Not even with those with whom he might've considered to be his closest friends.

"Have you given any thought as to what you'll do, Commander, after you capture the murderer?" she asked, biting into a plump strawberry. A little juice dribbled down her chin.

Robert reached out to dab at the juice with his handkerchief. Their hands touched and as he stared down at her lips, she thought he might kiss the trickle of juice away.

She handed him back his handkerchief and the moment passed.

"Oh—um, yes, before all this mayhem started, I had thought to buy myself a place to live somewhere near here. I was going to use my money and buy a cottage with a bit of land to farm," he said. "I intend one day to have a family."

A small wrinkle appeared on her brow, but inside, her heart cracked a little. So, he intended to marry.

"I suppose you will be in need of a proper English wife to go with this cottage of yours," she said, trying to keep the sadness from her voice.

If Lieutenant Smythe wanted to continue up the ranks of the Royal Navy, he would have to have a wife with the proper background and pedigree of respectability. An English lady with a title and a coffer full of shillings would be perfect for such an ambitious young officer.

Aye, she thought sorrowfully, a proper English wife with connections would be able to aid him, introduce him into the inner circles of polite society and help him advance his career. She would host and attend parties with him . . . and in due time bear his children. This esteemed lady would manage his farm while he was away at sea, ordering around the hired hands, selling the produce on market day, and on occasion be trusted to represent him in his absence. That is unless she decided to go to sea with him during times of peace. Aye, she would be a most respected member of society. Sarah envied this unknown woman.

She envisioned this proper English lady with her long aristocratic nose and white powdered hair. She would be a lady of decorum who would have undoubtedly all the manners and lofty airs of one of those brought up in the upper levels of society.

Aye, with his becoming good looks and manner, he could undoubtedly leg-shackle himself to a lady with a rich dowry, she sadly decided. And what would a poor wise woman such as herself have to offer him? Nothing. Not even a shilling. Aye, she could only afford to offer him herself. And no sensible gentleman with any ambition would want only her.

She looked over at him, her thoughts straying to their lovemaking.

She'd only had one glorious night with him, but how would it feel to be loved by him night after night as his wife? She could not help but wonder. Would he, like other seamen who were away from their loved ones for a long period of time, take a mistress? Or would he be true to his wife? Perhaps sending for her as often as he was able?

Maybe he would take an Irish mistress . . . a small

voice whispered inside her mind, *someone like you . . . maybe he would want an independent lady who would be both his companion as well as his lover?"*

However, would she be willing to be second in his life? Would she be content to let herself be available to him only as a source of momentary amusement?

Knowing the answer beforehand, she shook her head . . . she could not.

Robert took her hand in his, distracting her away from her sobering thoughts. He touched the gold ring she wore, moving it around on her finger as if its hidden love charm might rub off on him.

"But my plans might change," he said aloud. "Maybe she'll prefer a grand house in town and not want a country farm. Perhaps she'll have interests of her own such as cooking . . . or healing . . . and not desire to live here in England while I'm away at sea."

He looked down at her.

"There is a lot I would have to discuss with this lady. Such decisions a gentleman should not make alone."

He paused, letting his meaning sink in. "By the by, I'd like it if you'd call me Robert. I think it's high time that you did. That is, if it's acceptable to you . . . Sarah. I liked hearing your name on my lips last night, my sweet. I would hear it again."

He brought her hand up to his mouth and gently kissed it. Not content with that he peeled back the edges of her gloved hand, gently nibbling on the tender skin of her wrist.

She stared at him, blinked, almost afraid to breathe lest he should stop.

"I'll call you as you wish . . . ," she whispered, trying to focus, a haze of desire fogging her vision. "We are supposed to be betrothed. It would be, um . . . proper, Robert."

"It would indeed," he said, and bending towards her placed his other hand behind her back, pulling her closer to him.

He lowered his head and his mouth descended on hers.

It tasted of the fresh salt sea air and the sweets he had consumed during the celebrations. It piqued her hidden desires to be with him again and again. The gentle pressure of his mouth against her own felt oh, so wonderful. She leaned into him, wordlessly asking for more.

He tightened his hold.

It warmed her, making her head swim and all of her senses come alive. To be kissed, like this as a betrothed couple would, in front of all the crew and their families, by the man she had been yearning for these past few weeks, left her heady with happiness. The sobering recognition that he found her as attractive as she did him made her almost giddy.

He must have developed some tender feelings for her. She thought with a flutter of a butterfly in her stomach. And was he referring to her when he spoke of his future wife's interests? Or was it wishful thinking on her part?

Oh, how she wanted to ask him. Such intimate confidences made her hopeful. She wanted to love again. And be loved.

The gold ring was a constant reminder of her first love. She remembered the moment he'd given it to her. It had been when John Maxwell in his sweet fumbling way, asked her to be his wife.

There had been a purpose behind giving her the ring. And she knew it had nothing to do with a love charm. It was to remind her that she had loved and was capable of being loved in return. Although John was gone, and she grieved his loss, she knew she was able to go on living and feel those wonderful, tender emotions with someone else.

She no longer had to be alone. She did not have to live with only bittersweet memories to warm her. She could be part of the present and feel those heady sensations for another.

As Robert reached for her once more, to embrace her with another tender kiss, she knew in that moment all those wonderful hopes and promises a woman could have for one man. She placed her head against his shoulder and let him kiss her.

She was comforted by the thought that he had grown to care for her. Her feelings were not one sided. Maybe his affection for her would grow into something upon which they could build a future together. Perhaps he would ask her to continue to be by his side after they uncovered the identity of the murderer.

She put her hand on top of his. The ring shone in the moonlight. At that moment she felt safe with him and believed anything was possible between them . . . even love.

* * *

Suddenly, they heard a howling cry of feminine grief. It effectively broke the feeling of calm well-being to those celebrating aboard. A young woman cloaked in a long black ermine cloak stood at the top of the ship's gangplank.

Robert groaned inwardly. She had arrived.

Several officers of various ages were heard trying to dissuade her from coming aboard. But to no avail . . . she brushed them aside with forceful determination.

The young artist, Fiona Foxworthy, was famous for having tantrums at the slightest provocation. Sensitivity of feeling, an artistic temperament embraced by Lord Byron and his poetic friends, took on an entirely new meaning when the mercurial dancer was near. The

[143]

young dancer could make an old slattern seem placid by comparison.

Robert grimly remembered a past encounter with one of her hairbrushes. Fiona had thrown it at him after he'd bluntly turned down her offer to become one of her many admirers. He had other plans for his life and his money. The modest investments he'd made, he hoped would carry him through into old age. As a result of maintaining a tight-fist on his earnings, he'd earned the sorry reputation for being a tea-drinking-sober-sides. A man disinterested in wine, women, and song. That wasn't entirely true, though. There was one woman who had occupied his mind a great deal of late. He looked over at Sarah, who was watching the dancer's approach with great fascination. Sarah could make a man forget his very own name.

"I must see where my beloved Captain Jackson breathed his last—where he spent his final days . . . ," wailed the young woman, disregarding the fact that she'd already been told he had died upon a small island off the shores of southern Ireland.

"Step aside," she said imperiously to one of the young seamen who tried to dissuade her. She placed a hand dramatically across her brow and pushed him away with the other.

"I must commune with the air where he breathed his last words . . . I must touch where my beloved captain once laid his head to rest and be with those who knew him. Yes, I must be allowed to share my grief with all of those who served so valiantly with him!"

The beautiful young lady paused in her tirade. She looked about the top deck, trying to locate one of the ranked officers. It was evident she had come aboard to pay her respects. And she was not to be deterred from her mission.

She was in fact, looking for an officer to take

Captain Jackson's place as her protector. It would be a gentleman who would be as accommodating as her dear departed lover. He would therefore have to be someone who already knew of her whimsically demanding ways, someone who was close to the late captain and felt guilty for having survived . . . aye, someone like the handsome first mate.

She spied the newly appointed Master and Commander Robert Smythe.

Her painted lips pursed into a frown. A comely young woman with long guinea-colored hair had her hand clasped with the first officer's. This fact Fiona chose to ignore. She had heard rumors about his unconventional match with an Irish wise woman. No matter—she'd already decided upon her target.

"Yoo-hoo . . . Lieutenant Smythe!" Fiona cried, waving her handkerchief.

She effortlessly pulled away from her group of admirers, trailing behind her, and hurried up the steps to the officers' quarter-deck.

Robert gave a low groan of dismay and muttered a curse under his breath—the sort an officer did not utter in mixed company. But in this case, Sarah excused him. She thought of a few choice words of her own in Irish.

Their perfect evening had come to an abrupt end.

He gently disengaged himself from her and stood to politely greet the new arrival. It was sadly his duty to be kind to Captain Jackson's mistress in this, her hour of mourning.

"Mistress Foxworthy," he said as a short way of introduction for Sarah's benefit. "And this is my betrothed, wise woman Sarah Duncan."

Ignoring the young woman seated next to him, the dancer threw herself into the master commander's arms. She began to sob loudly, pushing her pretty face into his wool coat.

"My heart is broken." She sniffled into his chest. "Completely broken . . ."

Robert tried to gently extricate himself. But she was not to be moved. She clung to him, like a tenacious barnacle with sharp nails.

"He's gone, Lieutenant—left me all alone!" she cried out. "How could Captain Jackson leave me this way? How could he die, Lieutenant? And how shall I ever be comforted by his loss? I am so utterly alone in this cruel, cruel world. Whatever shall I do?"

By now a small group of her admirers stood at the bottom of the quarter-deck, looking up in adoration at the winsome vixen. A few of them, moved by her speech, softly uttered pledges to help her, to support her in her hour of grief.

"Darling Fiona, I'll take care of you," said one.

"Miss Foxworthy, you need never be alone again, Reginald dearest will provide," cried out another. One young fellow even went so far as to boldly declare, "I'll make you my wife, Fiona, and we'll live happily together, my dear!"

But this more serious declaration of love was met with outright anger. Several of the more senior admirers, who were married, gave the lovesick swain a hearty shove. In return, the offended young dandy delivered a perfectly aimed facer.

Sensing that a riot might occur and ignoring the fact that some of Fiona's admirers were higher ranking officers than him, Robert said loudly, "The next man to raise a hand will be put in the brig for a week! There's to be no fighting aboard this frigate."

Meaningfully, he eyed the gentlemen below.

"You are all my guests here. I will come after the first Jack man of you who puts a single toe out of line!"

He nodded to the two marines who were standing sentry by the captain's door. They descended and stood by the brawling gentlemen. Spirits quickly calmed at the sight of the bayonets the marines held.

Sarah directed her own attention at the cook. "Get the gentlemen some punch, Mr. Baker. They must be thirsty and in want of some hospitality. We must make them feel welcome with some good cheer."

"Aye, aye, Mistress Duncan." The old seaman grinned, winking up at her as he saluted her. He went off in search of some spirits for the lovesick gentlemen.

Fiona, as if all this attention and fuss were perfectly normal, dabbed her eyes with a white handkerchief. She sniffed prettily and patted one of her blonde curls back into place. Slowly, she removed herself from Robert's person. Her scene was finished.

The audience, with the exception of the commander and his betrothed, had responded exactly as she'd desired. It had all been most satisfactory.

She gave a smug smile to Sarah. She preened, thinking of how she would have her choice of protectors to choose from on the morrow. In a few weeks she would take off the mourning colors of black and gray, and once again become the fetching Venus of the Royal Naval Officer's Club.

Robert let loose a small sigh. What he did not need now was for one of these admiring senior officers to take it into their head to become jealous of him. He had enough trouble as it was. He didn't need to be labeled a seafaring Casanova and be connected with the hot-tempered, grieving vixen. Gently taking Sarah by the arm, he strategically placed her between himself and the calculating minx.

He planted a possessive hand about the wise woman's waist. It was a clear indicator as to where his affections lay. He was interested in one woman only, the winsome lady he wrapped his arm around.

The crew and group of admirers below noted this.

Aye, it wasn't the late Captain Jackson's mistress, the master and commander of The Brunswick would be spending his shore leave with, that was fair certain.

Fiona peeked around Sarah and looked at him. As if reading his thoughts, she made a face and whispered aloud, "Coward."

The vixen flounced over to the quarter-deck railing, surveying her small group of admirers. Deliberately, she released her handkerchief into the air and watched with a smug smile of satisfaction as it floated gently down to the deck below.

All eyes were upon the small white piece of cloth.

Mayhem ensued and an all-out brawl broke out.

Officers, regardless of rank, jumped upon other gentlemen, trying to elbow the others out of the way, seeking the small prize. Grunts and loud curses filled the air . . . until, with a howl of delight, a victor emerged.

A sprightly senior officer with almost six decades on him crawled out of the pile of flailing arms, legs, and hands. His white wig sat askew on his balding head. He stood up and brushed off his clothes and walked purposefully towards the quarter-deck with the sang-froid of a man used to doing battle.

He carried the white handkerchief aloft in one hand.

Eyeing the steps, he ascended them with the vigor of one half his years. Ignoring the venomous stares of the other gentlemen, he presented the handkerchief to the lovely Fiona.

"Oh, Rear Admiral, how gallant of you." The beauty simpered, placing a hand upon her heart. She batted her lashes at him, rewarding him with a gloved hand for him to kiss.

"It was nothing, my dear. Nothing at all." The elderly officer smiled, wiping his brow, before bending over the proffered hand. "May I escort you back to your carriage, Miss Foxworthy? I do believe the soiree here has come to an end."

"Please do, sir," the vixen said in an exaggerated grateful tone. "I am afraid I shall faint away if I stay here much longer. All of this attention has been most trying on my sensitive nerves."

She took his offered arm, calculating in her head how she might get the gentleman to help her. Perhaps he would be willing to cover the rent on her townhouse for the following two months? She did not know how it had happened, but all the money Captain Jackson had left to provide for her had seemingly slipped through her fingers.

Before parting, she turned and quickly planted a kiss upon Robert's cheek. Her eyes flashed triumphantly over at Sarah, her delight at having done so. Knowing full well it might cause an argument between them.

Fiona boldly added, "It was most excellent meeting you again, Lieutenant Smythe. I do hope you remember to send me anything that my dearly departed Captain Jackson might have bequeathed me. Perhaps he left some jewels, silk, silver, or blunt? If so, do send me word. I eagerly look forward to meeting you again, sir. And I hope it is very soon."

Sarah raised her eyebrows at that assumption.

The devil, she says! I'll scratch her eyes out first if she ever lays a finger upon him. She balled her hands into fists, ready to jump on the trollop if she came any closer.

As if reading her thoughts, Robert hugged her tightly to his side.

"If there should be something that comes to my attention, I'll have . . ." He paused giving it a moment's thought, looking down at the unmarried officers. "I'll have my second mate, Lieutenant Litton, bring it to you, Miss Foxworthy."

She in turn gave the second mate a sly smile.

[149]

The second mate, Lieutenant Litton, cut almost as dashing a figure as the master and commander in his uniform. And more importantly, his pockets were almost as well lined. He might do very well as a replacement for Captain Jackson.

"Yes-s," she lisped affectedly. "Please do send Lieutenant Litton, Commander."

With one final swish of her ermine trimmed cloak, she left the frigate.

Her small court of admirers trailed behind. When she reached the gang-plank, the men jostled for a better position near the beauty and in all the excitement, one of the swains fell into the harbor—a rope and barrel were tossed down so that he might not drown. It was, some said, a fitting end to the night's boisterous festivities.

Chapter 10

The next day the crew of The Brunswick was dismissed. Robert and Sarah left for the town of Portsmouth. The port was heavily protected by surrounding stone walls and cannons situated on top of high battlements.

The Royal Naval base was one of the most important in the British Empire, also one of the seediest, full of dens of iniquity. It was a typical seafaring town. Drunken sailors on leave and harbor trollops met openly on the cobbled streets in front of taverns.

Portsmouth was filled with the typical debauchery one would expect from seamen who had been too long contained in tight spaces without female companionship, or any other recourse of entertainment. Despite its air of open rowdiness, it played an important part in Britain's empire building. It was from this port that the fleet commanded by Lord Horatio Nelson went out and defeated Napoleon at Trafalgar.

But not all of the port was low-brow. There were, Sarah noted, on the High Street, several handsome new houses with shiny well-kept windows. Local vendors and shops were located nearby, catering their wares to the middle-class seamen and merchants.

Their carriage traveled away from these more elegant quarters, where officers and admirals dwelled. It ventured into one of the dark narrow streets, a place where abject poverty reigned. Sea harbor prostitutes and grog taverns plied their trade in the bowels of the poorest part of town.

It was in one of these narrow streets that they located number thirty-one, North Port Street. Here they found the rented rooms of the mysterious Mrs. Jemima Kaye.

"She came back from one of her wanderings a few days ago, Lieutenant," said an old woman, wiping her nose with the back sleeve of her blouse.

She wore a dirty dust cap with tattered lace that dangled down one side of her graying hair. As Robert and Sarah drew closer, the old woman's rum-soaked breath threatened to overwhelm their nostrils. The woman took a gulp from a flask dangling from her hip and gave them a speculative look.

"She takes off for months at a time, ever since that wretched husband of hers died. But then she always comes back 'ere in good time. She recommended Old Nancy's place to you two, did she? Ye want to rent a room?" she asked. "Mine are plenty clean enough for an hour or so of fun . . . that is for them who desire to be alone with a pretty gel, such as you have there, guv'nor."

She gave them a suggestive toss of the head towards her establishment. Greasy, streaked windows looked down upon the street. A sooty alley cat lazily meowed as it rolled over on the dirty stoop. The house looked to be on the verge of collapse. It leaned to one side with large wooden beams propped beneath the walls on the right to brace it.

"I'm thinking maybe I could even give you a cut-rate price. That is, if you was to let the young lady 'ere walk the streets tonight with me gels. Why, I'd even promise to take care of her once you got back to your ship, Commander." The whoremonger beamed. "I'd make right certain she'd be safe and dry whilst you were gone.

And if anything should happen to you . . ." She left a significant pause, eyeing the ring Sarah wore. "Well, to be sure, I'll see to it myself that she'd find another husband to watch out for her, Lieutenant."

"I have no doubt," said Robert dryly.

He glanced upwards at a group of women who were of all ages, standing by the windows in various stages of dishabille. These ladies of the night worked for Old Nancy and hung out the different windows of the establishment, displaying their exposed flesh.

One or two of the women, without any great enthusiasm, lifted their light skirts to show him their shapely legs and garters. Another, a blonde woman of Rubenesque proportions, was so bold as to pull back her paisley shawl and thrust forward her tightly corseted bosom. It was a wonder her breasts did not spill out of the garment, the strain on the laces being so great.

"Not interested in any o' them, are ye, sir? Sure ye won't take one of me clean rooms off me hands for an hour or two?" Old Nancy asked, scratching a series of small red welts on her plump arms, the result of the establishment's linens being undoubtedly infested with bed bugs.

"No," he repeated.

He produced two silver guineas from his money purse. "I want some more information about your tenant, Mrs. Kaye—and anyone else who might have lived with her."

Old Nancy reached out a gloved hand to greedily take the guineas from him. He quickly moved them out of her reach.

"The information first," he said softly with a small, tight smile.

Eyeing the coins, Old Nancy nodded. Her eyes fixed themselves upon the coins he held. She was more than willing to give him the information he sought.

"Right, well before she became Mrs. Kaye, our

Jemima, was one of me gels. A good worker she was. Officers and captains were eating out o' her hands. Peculiar though about who she took to her room. But she was still mighty popular with the gents. She was almost as handsome a looker as that one there," she said, nodding her head at Sarah, "'til she took to being ever so peculiar."

The woman shook her straggly, gray curls.

"Jemima said her mother had once been a maid in the Spanish royal court and her father, a French merchant—but they both got drowned at sea, so she said." Nancy paused in her tale, wiping her nose on the sleeve of her gown. "She came here to live with me and make her living after their deaths."

"A year ago she took up with a foreign bloke by the name of Kaye. A dangerous fellow, he was, I can tell ye, Commander. He gave me the shivers, he did. Eyes like cold steel he had when he looked at ye, sir. And the men he brought with him were of the worst sort. Aye, none of me gels wanted to have anything to do with that rough lot. A right gang of cutthroats, they were. Scary, if ye get my meaning."

"Did Jemima suddenly disappear with these men?" asked Sarah, thinking the woman might have been taken away by force from the house of ill repute.

"Nay," spat Old Nancy, "she weren't kidnapped if that what ye be thinking. Something worse than that occurred."

She grimaced and spat into the street.

"She leg-shackled herself to Kaye. Up and married him, she did. She started putting on more airs than a drunken fairy walking about in her nightdress. Huh! Her who used to walk the streets with me others, telling us how to behave . . . but then a few months after the wedding, she came back out of the blue. She wanted her old room back and her money purse was full to the brim with blunt. Not that she gave Old Nancy any."

"Was he with her?" asked Robert.

"Nay," said Nancy, shaking her gray head.

"She came back alone and started drinking and cussing. She was wearing black widow's weeds when she returned . . . apparently that cur she married had managed to get himself killed at sea." She shrugged and said. "No surprise there, what with the dreadful company that one kept. Pirates and blockade runners, they all were. And I told her myself that she was better off without him. But the gel did pine so for that black-hearted devil."

"What happened after she returned?" Robert asked, shining the guineas on his coat sleeve. "Did she perchance have a son named Jeremy?"

"Jeremy?" repeated the brothel owner. "Nay, Jemima never had any children. She's got no living relations to speak of, that I know of, gov'nor. The man is probably just one of her lovers. She never was too picky about the age of the men she bedded. Just so long as he had the airs and blunt of a wealthy nob. Nay, she used to have a go at all of the puffed up gentlemen at one time or another."

"I'd like to see her room," he said quietly, so that the other women nearby could not overhear his words.

Old Nancy lifted her eyebrows at him. She eyed his leather pouch, which hung by his side. Aloud, she said, "You say ye wish to use one of me rooms, Commander? Two guineas, that'll cost ye."

He dropped the guineas into her hand. Her red-rimmed eyes lit up.

"Very well, follow me," she said, tapping her pipe on the railing before opening the warped front door.

They obediently followed. The brothel owner's broad backside swayed as she walked, going up and down, mimicking waves at sea. Although midday, the interior of the house was dark and dank. Cooked food and gentleman's tobacco permeated the air. Dust mites floated in thick clouds in what little sunlight had managed to enter the old building.

They stepped onto tattered carpets, the floorboards creaking with every step. They walked up a narrow flight of stairs to the bedchambers above.

The inhabitants, ladies in their light under skirts and corsets lined up by their bedchamber doors to look the couple over. Hands on hips, they observed them.

Sarah's cheeks reddened at some of the suggestive remarks directed at Lieutenant Smythe. She had never heard such explicit talk.

"If she gets boring, I'm just next door, love," cooed the tightly corseted blonde at Robert. She batted her eyelashes suggestively at him before giving him a wink.

Another, an Irish trollop with freckles, smirked after looking over Sarah's trim frame.

"If ye find she's got something not quite right, come on over. We can have a wee bit o' fun together . . . I'll give you a bit of a tickle for sure to please all your fancies."

"I wouldna even charge ye a pence, if you were mine," put in another, the oldest working lady present. So emaciated and ill looking was her appearance, she looked to be on her way to the pearly gates. "It'd be a real pleasure, Commander."

Sarah could tell this harlot was in her last days. The light-skirt might in reality be in her early twenties for all one could tell, but the soiled dove's flesh was rotting fast and she looked vastly older than her years.

The smell of opium emitted from the prostitute's room as she passed. Oblivion had its rewards. Sarah paused, noticing a small painted portrait of a seaman on the bureau and the smoking hookah next to it.

"He was my husband," the woman said with a toss of her head. "What little good it did me. When he died, I lost everything."

Sarah did not dare ask what she meant by "everything." She had heard enough from widowed women abandoned by seafaring husbands and seen starving orphaned children dying in dank back rooms. This lady's story would be no different or unique than the others. It would even end the same way, with an untimely death.

Sarah carefully hid the pity she felt. She knew by the fierce look in the woman's eyes that she would resent it. What little pride the woman had managed to retain and what disdain she felt towards those whose lives were more fortunate than her own, could cause the soiled dove to become vicious and spiteful.

There had unfortunately been times in the past when Sarah had been attacked. She had learned to be prudent with her compassion. She said nothing to the woman as she walked by her.

"Enough of this chatting," said Old Nancy pointedly to the ladies of the house. "You lot either are abed sleeping one off or out getting yourself a customer . . . and if I see any of you ladies watching these two, I'll have ye out in the streets with the rest of the gutter snipes—ye hear? Now get off with you."

"All right, Nance, no need to get your knickers bunched up. You know we always do what ye tell us to," said one of the women, throwing a shawl over her shoulders in a slight huff.

The ladies docilely returned to their rooms and their beds. Old Nancy might be a right nasty cow, but working for her was a lot better than being alone and out on the cold wet streets of Portsmouth.

Doors were heard closing and a few of the ladies could be heard flopping back onto their beds in preparation for the long evening ahead. The women knew that if they didn't contribute some shillings, they would quickly find themselves kicked-out. Sleeping in the cold was not desirable. At least in this rundown boarding house, they had a bed to call their own and regular meals to fill their bellies. Aye, it was better than no place at all.

Old Nancy unlocked the door to Jemima Kaye's bedchamber with a heavy key.

Sarah suspected this wasn't the first time the down-at-the-heel brothel owner had rented the room when the original renter was absent. None of the other ladies had said a word about Old Nancy letting the couple use Jemima's room in her absence. This apparently was routine.

The room was sparse with a rickety chair, a scratched roll top writing desk and a small single bed. A smudged window, streaked with soot, looked out onto the back alley and the brick wall of the building next door.

"I'll give you two some time alone," said Old Nancy, giving a significant sideways glance at the writing desk.

From the sly glance she gave them, Sarah surmised that the old brothel owner had already taken a look herself. It didn't look like it would be difficult to do. A pen-knife would easily open the desk's flimsy lock.

The moment she closed the door behind her, Robert opened the desk. A neat pile of writing paper was stacked on the upper right hand part of the desk, an ink well situated next to it.

"Examine the letters. We might learn something from any past correspondence she may have had with Jeremy," he said, nodding at the letters written on cheap parchment paper.

Going quickly through them, Sarah scanned them for Jeremy's name. Robert busied himself with opening the lower drawers.

"Nothing," he said, flipping through what looked like a pile of old gazettes. They listed the various brothels and their occupants in Portsmouth, including this one.

One of the gazettes was Harris's listing of Covent Garden Demimonde Courtesans and Prostitutes, a lively description of the harbor trollops living around Portsmouth. Many descriptions were given in nautical terms. Several hundred ladies, bawdy establishments, taverns, and brothels were listed. Prostitution was a thriving trade, setup to part bored, lonely seamen and merchant sailors from their hard earned wages.

Jemima had circled her own listing.

"She lists herself as a lover of the sons of Neptune," said Sarah, reading aloud the gazette entry. "She's been working for the past four years as a harlot and it states that not a Jack-man has been the worse for knowing her. Although in her early thirties, many a shipmate has found her company to be most agreeable and easy to board for an afternoon of pleasuring . . . her islet being narrow enough to accommodate—"

She abruptly stopped in her reading. She was slightly embarrassed by the lyrical seaman's jargon that went on to describe the prostitute's body in detail.

"And it, um, lists her fee . . . at the time she was available for thirty shillings."

"A modest sum, a fee almost any ordinary seaman could have afforded. And from what Old Nancy told us," commented Robert sardonically, "I suspect her price went up considerably once she met Kaye. She probably no longer needed or desired to work that trade. That is if she continued whoring after falling in love with the dangerous rogue."

"I suppose so," murmured Sarah, thoughtfully closing the gazette.

She tried not to think of what it must have been like for the woman to return to this lowly place after her husband's untimely death. It would have been disheartening.

Aloud, she said, "For Jemima it must have been shameful to come back here . . . especially as she probably thought she would never have to return to this place. It was no wonder she took to drink. It undoubtedly helped her numb herself to having to come back here."

She looked over the room. It felt cold and impersonal. There was very little warmth or comfort to offer its occupant.

"Aha!" he said significantly, drawing out a playbill for a tavern. It had an ink drawing of a woman standing on stage in a gaudy, revealing costume.

He pointed to it. "Look . . . Jemima Kaye will be appearing here tonight direct from her Dublin debut."

"She sings?" she asked, looking over his shoulder.

She took a good look at the singer. There was something about the performer that nagged at the back of her thoughts with an eerie sense of déjà-vu . . . they had met before, she was certain of it. She tried to remember. She could not place it. Perhaps Jemima had been in Ireland once? But when had they met?

"Our queen of song has appeared in all the great cities of the United Kingdom. And it says here, 'For your pleasure, gents, we've retained her charming self for your viewing.'"

He handed her the playbill.

"The Hair of the Dog Tavern—that's where we'll find her."

"It sounds disreputable and dangerous. But we're going to pay it a visit, aren't we, Robert?"

He raised an eyebrow at her. "I'm going to pay it a visit, yes."

"No, we are going together," she countered.

He frowned, shaking his head.

At his stern look of disapproval, she said with grim determination, "I have run into the ghost of a murdered seaman, been frightened out of my wits by a possible murderer, and viewed the corpse of a dead man. I repeat, sir, there is nothing that would keep me from this venture of hunting down Jeremy. I have the right to know what happened as much as you do."

"But the men we may encounter might be unsavory characters, Sarah. I—"

"Cutthroats, low-lifes, in other words, the devil's own men," she said, nodding in emphatic agreement. "The sort you'll be after telling me a lady shouldn't be exposed to . . . aye, I understand, and in any other circumstance undoubtedly I would agree with you. But then, when in my entire life have I ever been considered by society to be respectable and proper?"

He opened his mouth to give a rebuttal, but she cut him short.

"Aye, I know you think a wise woman, such as I, has never been exposed to this less savory side of life. But I have. Indeed I've treated all sorts of ruffians. Some of whom I may add were not the least bit grateful for the help I gave. I've been in places a saner person would have refused to step into, and yet I've come out alive. Nay, there's no reason to leave me behind, Robert."

Her blue eyes sparkled with resolve. She was determined to follow him wherever this mystery might take them. She wanted to remain by his side.

He in turn smiled down at her. He moved closer, making her very aware of his attractive manliness. "But there is a reason you should not go, my dear. You see, I would rather fillet the first man who would dare to lay a finger on you with my own knife, than be promoted to first admiral of the king's navy. I am that fond of you, Sarah."

"Oh," she said, eyes widened at his confession.

"Oh, indeed," he echoed.

She rewarded him with a smile.

"Faith, it does seem rather a perilous course,

Lieutenant, and to think I was that determined to go with you, too."

"But you won't go now, will you? You'll do this favor for me, won't you?" he asked, gently taking her hand into his.

He drew her over to the single bed.

They sat down. Their eyes on each other's face, caught up in the emotions of two lovers drawn to each other by forces that had nothing to do with duty, ambition, or common sense—but had everything to do with mutual attraction and feelings of tender, warm affection.

"I'll stay behind if that is what ye wish," she said, reluctantly letting him win the argument. She squeezed his hand.

"It is," he said firmly.

He looked down at her rosy lips. They parted slightly, invitingly . . . Unable to resist any further her winsome charms, he kissed her. It was full of sunny tenderness. It warmed them both, causing them to forget their rough surroundings and reason for being there. They forgot everything and everyone, only concerned with each other and their need to be close.

Robert's mouth descended on hers and the warmth she'd experienced on the night of the betrothal party filled her again as he nibbled on her lower lip, his hands boldly plundering the front of her bodice, beneath her comfy shawl. He murmured endearments in her ear, while gently rubbing the nipples of her breasts, kissing her.

"Oh, Robert," she said softly, desiring more of his touch, wanting to continue exploring each other.

Breathing hard, he drew back and, looking around at the unsavory surroundings they found themselves in, said, "We shall have to continue this at another time."

He planted a quick kiss on her forehead, resisting

the temptation to continue, drawing the shawl she wore back around her shoulders.

A loud knock rapped on the door.

Old Nancy ambled into the room. She looked at them and shook her head disapprovingly.

"If ye want this room longer, Commander Smythe," she said. "That'll be another two guineas you'll owe me. I run a proper brothel here, not some charity for cupid. And you two best be hoisting anchor and leave the premises before she returns. Jemima won't take kindly to seeing you two aboard her bed."

"Aye, aye." Robert saluted the old woman mockingly.

Laughing, they hastily rose and left the house of ill repute and its residents far behind.

Chapter 11

The Hair of The Dog Tavern was without a doubt the seediest and most dangerous place Robert had ever stepped foot in. By the look of the men inside, it was questionable that even an ordinary seaman would have had the foolishness to poke his face into such a dangerous place.

Any decent man who stepped in here had best have no fear of dubious backgrounds and evil characters, thought Robert, looking over the tavern's cavernous room.

Newgate Prison's punishing bleak interior was not unknown to the patrons inside. The people who sat around the rough wooden tables laughing and joking were gamblers, robbers, and loose women. It would not have surprised Robert to know that members of the black-market, pirates, kidnappers, and paid assassins, as well as other evil assorted mercenaries, lingered over tankards, in the darker corners.

On the tavern's small stage, surrounded by smoking footlights, sat a young woman in a red-velvet, high-backed chair. Wearing a gaudy costume made of flashy green liberty silk and torn lace, the song bird was in the middle of singing *Charlotte, the Harlot* a bawdy sea shanty, to the accompaniment of an accordion she held in her hands.

Her legs were spread wide like a man's. One was swung over an arm of the chair. It kicked out in time with the music and as it did so several men let out catcalls and high-pitched whistles of appreciation.

She wore no modest bloomers. Her shapely legs were completely exposed up to her thighs. The audience could spot the red garters she wore to keep her black-netted stockings up.

The singer's low alto voice was not particularly good. But it could be heard over the raucous noise. This undoubtedly was why the owner of the tavern had hired her. It certainly wasn't for her taste in music. The songs she sang were raunchy ditties sung in the form of well-known sea chanteys, allowing the patrons to join her in the familiar choruses with their own warbling drunk voices.

Robert had chosen to disguise himself as the first mate of a merchant ship running illegal rum. It would not do to look as if he were in any way connected with the English government. Not unless he wished to have his throat slit.

He had carefully chosen to wear a seaman's wool overcoat, minus its insignia and a long dark blue cap, the sort French sailors wore. His clothes gave him the air of one who had spent a lot of time away from England. He had not shaved that day and rough stubble covered his jaw.

In the dark smoky lights of the tavern room, he could not make out Jemima Kaye's face, only her form and voice.

Making a slow circuit through the crowded room, he went up to the bar.

"What do ye want?" asked the barman, a bald man wearing a long white apron, wiping a wet spot in front of him.

"A tankard o' your darkest brew," he said, placing a shilling down.

The ale was placed before him.

He took it and made his way up to the tables located nearest the stage. He stood in the shadows of the tavern walls, catching his first glimpse of the face of the woman performing.

Illuminated by the stage lights, he saw a familiar face, one he had not expected to see . . . it was Jeremy! The singer on stage, Mrs. Jemima Kaye, was the young deserter.

He looked again, not quite believing his eyes.

But it was true. Mrs. Jemima Kaye, the widow of a sea captain with nasty acquaintances, was also the young seaman and suspected murderer of the steward. She was none other than Jeremy Kaye.

He gagged on his ale, spilling some of the brew onto the sawdust-covered floor. Numbly, he sat down on a bench by the back wall. In the shadows he watched with fascination the woman who had successfully disguised herself as an ordinary seaman.

Taking inventory of her features and physical aspects, he could discern the well-formed muscles of a seaman's arms as they pumped the accordion in front of her. Her bared limbs were without a doubt those of a topsails man used to climbing up and down the riggings of a three-mast frigate.

Not being large breasted, he imagined how easy it must have been for her to flatten her breasts by wrapping linens tightly around herself. She had successfully disguised her feminine hips and curves by wearing baggy breeches, successfully hiding all evidence of her true sex. Jemima's black hair was naturally curly. At present, on stage, she wore long colorful peacock feathers stuck into them with a silk scarf tying it back. Aboard The Brunswick, she had worn a concealing fisherman's cap.

He recognized in the oval face what Sarah had first remarked upon when first meeting the young seaman, Jeremy . . . that he was a "pretty youth." But the grim line of Jemima's painted red mouth was set in an insolent manner.

She silently gave a cool look to those observing her.

It was as if she said, 'What do you think you're looking

at? You're no better than I am. And you sure as the devil are not manly enough to handle someone like me.'

Robert shook his head again in disbelief.

How had he been fooled? Why hadn't he noticed before the belligerent regard in which she looked at everyone, including him? How had it been she failed to escape his notice for so long? He had always prided himself on the attention he paid to his crew.

There was, he had to admit, a simple enough explanation. She had not before been important enough to merit his attention.

As long as ordinary seaman Jeremy Kaye never faltered at his job as a topsails man, there had never been any reason for him to speak to her. His second in command and the petty officers would have been the ones in direct contact with her, passing down the orders.

If she stayed out of their way and did her duty, there had been no reason to scrutinize any of Jemima's actions. It had apparently been quite easy to conceal her true identity from the ship's masters, as well as the ranked officers who served aboard.

What reason would anyone aboard have had for doubting her identity if she did her duty correctly? None whatsoever . . .

Aye, the revelation concerning Jeremy's true sex explained a myriad of mysteries about the deserter. Starting with the obvious reason the ordinary seaman had been shy and prudish about taking his clothes off to his aloof top-lofty attitude towards the entire crew. And this all added up to the obvious reason why she had never revealed anything about her personal life ashore to anyone.

He had many questions spinning around in his thoughts. Some which only Jemima could answer. What had made her decide to become a seaman? To what purpose had she planted herself amongst his crew? Had it been a personal reason, a private vendetta? And more importantly had she been the one to poison Captain Jackson and murder the steward, Stafford? If it was not her, then who?

He looked up at her at the moment she broke into another bawdy ditty.

Or maybe she had come aboard for another reason altogether? One he had not yet thought of. One perhaps only another woman would understand.

The revelation of her hidden sex brought to his thoughts tales of such ladies serving aboard British naval ships in disguise. Some women had been known to disguise themselves as seamen because they had a lover serving aboard.

Other ladies had done so out of sheer desperation. In order to earn money, food, and passage home after being widowed, abandoned, or shipwrecked. And there had been a daring few who had done so simply because they wanted to be seamen. They did so in order to earn an honest day's wages instead of working as a servant or harbor prostitute.

He looked back uneasily at Jemima's painted red mouth and shook his head.

Nay, the last assumption couldn't be right. She had not come aboard The Brunswick because she had wanted to be an ordinary seaman. With her, he sensed, it had to have been something more complicated and personal.

There was, he noted, something unsettling and mercenary about Jemima Kaye. The singer's features, her dark eyes, hair, and the curves of her hips and breasts which made up her body were pretty and feminine. Aye, she was not some desperate scrawny lass looking for a patron. She could have her pick among many seamen, including he imagined, officers in his majesty's navy.

However, that chillingly unpleasant sneer troubled

him. Something was not quite ordinary about her. There was an uncontrolled passion in those eyes. It was most unsettling.

When Jemima took her rest, he stepped out of the shadows and made himself known. Robert stood in front of the smoking lamp lights that lit the small wood stage.

She recognized him straight away.

"Oh, it be you, Lieutenant Smythe," she said eyeing him over. "So you've tracked me down at last. I suppose you want to talk to me about Stafford."

"Aye, I do," he said, stunned by her overconfident manner, the way her dark eyes flashed at him coolly meeting his stern look. "Where can we meet?"

"After I'm done singing here . . . meet me in the front alley in an hour. By then I should be finished amusing this lot."

The look she gave him sent a prickling warning shiver down his spine. It was the sort of sensation he had experienced once upon maneuvering a heavy bottomed third-rated ship of the line through sharp, hull-tearing reefs. An innate sixth sense told him to be wary. It was a clear sailor bewares sensation. And he, an experienced seaman, impetuously decided not to take heed.

"By the by, Commander . . . come alone," she said, dismissing him with a shrug of one of her muscled shoulders, "or don't bother to come at all."

He nodded, agreeing. It was a mistake he would later regret.

*　　*　　*

Sarah restlessly paced the quarter-deck of The Brunswick waiting for his return. Something was amiss, she sensed it. She should have gone with him, or at the very least followed at a distance. He had promised to be aboard before the next high tide. And that had come and gone an hour ago.

The devil take it, where was he? Why hadn't he returned as promised?

She remembered the face of the dead steward's ghost in the hull. The feeling of something dreadful having occurred, nagged at the back of her thoughts, leaving her numb and cold. She rubbed her arms for warmth.

Her fancies of what could have happened to Robert were running away with her. *Get a hold of yourself, Sarah, or you'll be of no use to him. If he is in trouble, you cannot fall to pieces with fear,* she reprimanded herself, her eyes scanning the dock for any sign of his approach.

He did not appear.

One hour later a single lantern glowed in the evening sea fog. She saw its approach in a blur. She had briefly fallen asleep on the top deck with a blanket wrapped about her. She had been sitting in the same chair that Captain Jackson had once occupied when ill, waiting.

The light came from a small quarter boat approaching the frigate by water. A large giant of a man was putting his back into rowing. A ship's lantern swung from a hook at the bow.

She peered out. It was Master O' Grady and someone else was with him.

At first she did not recognize who the other man was. His bent form was wrapped in a blanket and propped up against a potato sack. The man appeared to be asleep or dead drunk for he made no movements.

The giant tied the small boat to the dock. He then bent over and slung the other man over his broad shoulders, carefully walking up the gangplank.

She hurried to greet him, wondering which of the crew he carried. She did not have long to find out. Upon gazing at the bruised face of the man O'Grady carried on his shoulder, she let out a gasp of instant recognition.

"Robert . . . and he's been beaten!"

"Aye, ma'am," said the giant, nodding. "Best take him to the captain's cabin to lie him down. He's badly hurt."

She led the way to the cabin, opening the door for him. The master gunner lay his commander down on the narrow bed. He turned to her.

"For sure now, he's in a bad way, ma'am. Do ye think you can help him?" he asked. "Or do ye want me to fetch a surgeon?"

"No, I can take care of him," she said softly, looking at the mass of bruises marring the first lieutenant's face.

She turned and without wasting time on futile questions went to fetch the medicines she carried in her sea chest. Grabbing a handful of herbs and bottles, she set about doing what she knew best, healing.

Mrs. O'Grady, having been woken out of her slumber by her eldest son who'd been on watch, appeared by her side.

"What can I do to help?" the gentle Irish woman asked, her brow wrinkling at the horrible sight of the wounded man.

"Fetch some strong spirits, cold water, and clean linens," Sarah said, gently feeling about his head to see if his skull had been cracked open.

Thank the heavens above, she inwardly sighed with relief, the skull was intact.

A bad lump with a marring bruise appeared at the base. It had undoubtedly been brought about by the blow that had caused his senses to leave. She noted that his breathing was strong and even . . . another good sign. Perhaps if he was fortunate, none of his innards had been harmed.

"Open his shirt for me, Master O'Grady," she said, as she ran her hand skillfully down his legs, arms, and chest, feeling for any broken bones, almost afraid to discover what other harm had been done.

Robert bore dark blue bruises and fresh red scrapes

all over his body. He had been horribly thrashed. Whoever had done this, she doubted not, had done so with the evil intent of leaving him for dead. He was truly blessed to be alive.

The remainder of the night was a restless one for both healer and patient. Fearful he would fall into a deep unending sleep, she awakened Robert several times and forced him to walk around. In the early morning hours, as the sun appeared on the horizon, he regained consciousness.

In the morning Robert could not recall the fight that had brought about his present downfall. A sharp pain throbbed at the back of his skull and spread to the front of his temple.

He placed a hand on the large lump at the base of his neck and looked about. He tried to get his bearings. What was he doing lying in the captain's cabin instead of his own?

"Where am I? What happened to me? Ouch . . . I feel as if a boom was dropped on me. Is that what happened?"

He made an effort to rise, but nausea overtook him. He swayed back onto the bunk.

"The Brunswick, how is she? Did we go through a tempest gale? My crew—are all hands safe? And why are you here, Sarah?"

"Do not worry. Everything is right as rain. The Brunswick is safe and secure at port. The crew was dismissed two days ago. We're tied up to the dock in Portsmouth. Don't you remember?"

He tried to rise, but could not.

"Lie down. You've taken a bad beating," she said. She filled a cup of steaming bitter-root tea and passed it to him.

"Here, drink this . . . it may ease some of the pain. You're most fortunate to be alive."

"Do you know what happened to me?" he asked.

She shook her head. Though she wished to heavens

she had been there. She would like to have had the pleasure of trying to stick her own knife in the assailants.

"I only know that last night Master O'Grady brought you aboard in this well-hammered condition. You've been in and out of consciousness most of the night and this is the sixth time you've asked me what happened." She frowned. "I've had to waken you myself several times during the night to be sure that you hadn't fallen into a deep slumber . . . the sort I wouldn't be able to awaken you from."

Concerned, she asked, "Do you remember anything at all of last night? Do you remember searching for Jemima Kaye at this tavern?" she asked, showing him the flyer.

"Nay," he said, shaking his head. "I'm as blank as a piece of unwritten parchment. I can recall nothing of what happened or how I came to be in this lamentable condition."

"Do you want me to fetch Master O'Grady?" she asked, pressing a cold compress to the back of his head. "He may be able to tell you something of what occurred. It would appear that he was present when this took place."

"Nay, not if I am to go by the splendid bump on the back of my head. I must have caused him and his dear wife a great deal of trouble and worry. No, let them rest. I am certain they will deserve my thanks in the morn for whatever part Master O'Grady played in seeing me safely returned here."

He gently took her hand in his, appreciating her concern for him.

Not for a minute did he doubt that under her tender care he would soon return to his normal self. Having her calming presence beside him already made him feel better. She had the ability to turn the darkest situation

[173]

into one of hope. It was one of her healing qualities, which he liked and had come to value. For the moment, with his head pounding and his body aching, she was the only light in his dark, addled thoughts.

*   *   *

"It's good to see some color back in your face, Commander," said the giant master gunner, pulling on his forelock out of respect as he entered. His wife stood beside him anxious to see if the commander was on the mend.

"Aye, you're lookin' much better, sir," seconded his wife, taking a quick peek at him.

O'Grady bowed his head a little, trying not to hit it against the low cabin ceiling.

"To tell the truth, afraid for ye, was I, Commander. You were nigh almost a goner when I found you in that alley with those demon cutthroats. Aye, though it is certain ye must've put up one Jim-dandy of a fight against them to have come out alive like you did, sir."

He spared a glance in Sarah's direction. She silently shook her head.

"Oh," continued the giant softly, a look of compassion passing over his large features. "Aye, to be sure, I'd forgotten. The Mistress did tell me that you didn't remember what had happened to you. A grand shame that . . ."

"Tell me now, O' Grady. How did it come about that you found me? I take it I was unconscious?" asked Robert, reaching once more for the cold compress beside him.

He could smell the pungent lavender and clean spirits as he lifted it to his head. Sarah had made the poultice to help clear his muddled head. He pressed it to his temple and lay back again. Nausea once more swept across his insides. He fought the urge to be sick.

"Aye, you discerned correct, Commander." The master

[174]

gunner nodded. "I normally avoid that part of town. But my wife's sister has fallen upon hard times since her husband's death and took up lodging near there. I went to visit our daughter who has been living with her."

He grimaced in remembrance.

"I can only describe this place as a corner of the world belonging to Lucifer himself, sir. Mind I plan to set my daughter and her aunt up in a cozy cottage in the country as soon as I'm able. Aye, well, it was as I was going past this alley by The Hair of The Dog that I heard a commotion. I turned and in horror watched as some ugly tall bloke hit you, sir. He did so with a bottle. Then I saw . . ." O' Grady hesitated, he still had not quite believed his eyes. But noting the intense interest in his two listeners, he continued on with his tale.

He stated simply, "I saw Jeremy, sir. At least ways I believe it was him, for he was dressed in the attire of a female. He, I mean, she . . . well, she was yelling and screaming at the top of her lungs at them cutthroats, urging them into action. She wanted them to kill you right away, sir. Villainous, it was."

The gunner scratched the back of his neck in reflection.

"What followed was a wee bit of a blur, sir. I pulled myself together and entered the alley as one of those rapscallions was about to lay into you with a knife. I picked him right up and threw him head first against a nearby wall, knocking him out."

The giant demonstrated the throw with his long brawny arms. His large muscles, the same ones he used working the heavy forge on a daily basis, flexed as he made the motions.

"And then I took the other scurvy rat . . . he was a bucktoothed, skinny fellow that was standing next to you. He had a lead pipe in his hands ready to smash yer bones up with, he did, the rotter. Well, him I simply picked up by his boot straps and tossed him into the gutter with the rest of the horrid filth. He landed there and didn't budge, I'm glad to say, sir."

"As for yourself, you showed you were no yellow-tailed coward, sir. You'd already taken down one of them four scalawags before I got there, another you laid out with a good right hook to the jaw before a third hit ye in the back with a club, Commander."

"But what of Jemima? What did she do?" asked Sarah, her hands clenching her skirt, outraged by the thought of evil scoundrels trying to hurt Robert.

"She came at me like a wild cat, that one did," said O' Grady, pointing to a series of small scratches that ran down his sun-tanned cheeks.

His wife leaned over and kissed the scratch and said, "Brave man that you are."

"She was after your blood, sir. I must confess I wasn't sure what to do about her. I swear, ma'am, I've never laid a finger against a female before in my entire life. And this time I wouldn't have done it if she had not been set on destroying our good commander. She was ready to poke him herself with a blade that she had gripped in her hand."

"You do credit to your mother, Master O' Grady," Sarah commented, calmly reassuring him that whatever he did must have been done for the side of good—not evil.

"Aye, that he does," agreed his wife, beaming a smile of approval up at her giant of a husband as she hugged his side.

"But you know, sir, she was no lady you were holding at bay," added Sarah. "Gentlemanly restraint cannot be expected to be fair for everyone, especially when such as Jemima Kaye is hell-bent on seeing you killed. Aye, it is best to be after taking care not to have any harm come to yourself first than worrying over behaving properly to an evil viper such as her."

"Aye, that's for sure, Mistress. Musha, to think she and I were once shipmates, sharing the same food, drinking and working together. Aye, it makes my head swim to think of it. How for weeks she fooled all of us concerning her true sex and reasons for being aboard The Brunswick. It is all confusing."

He turned to Robert with an inquiring look.

"Did you know about her, sir? Is that why you were in that alley where I found you? Was it because of that hellion, sir?"

The officer nodded, slowly answering, "Aye . . . I remember vaguely seeing a woman who reminded me of someone. She was singing in the tavern—a terrible ditty—and playing an accordion. When I saw her face—" His face brightened, he suddenly remembered what happened. "That's it! I recognized her immediately as our missing Jeremy!"

He touched the lump at the back of his head gingerly.

"I think I must have decided to have a word with her. We talked briefly, that much I remember. She told me that she would meet me outside . . . alone. I went out and after that . . ." He left the thought unfinished, shaking his head, unable to recall what had happened next.

"I don't remember. It must be that when I stepped outside, she had already arranged for those scalawags to put an end to me."

He held out his hand to his master gunner.

"I owe you my life, O'Grady. If you hadn't found me, it is certain I wouldn't be here today. Instead, I would be yet another unexplained corpse left in a dark alley to be dropped into a gravedigger's ditch."

The gunner, his head humbly bowed by the compliment, shook Robert's hand.

"It was my pleasure, to be of some service to you, sir. You're a fine officer, Lieutenant. And I'd not be ashamed to serve under you once more if you were to be once again commander of The Brunswick. Aye, ye did a splendid job with both her and the crew. 'Tis certain it'll be a grand day for all of us when the Admiralty promotes you to the full rank of captain, sir."

"But what of Jemima Kaye?" Sarah asked. "What became of her? Did ye hand her over to the redcoats, Master O' Grady?"

"Nay, I didn't have the chance." The giant shook his head. "She kicked me in an unmentionable place and I dropped her. After which she took off at a quick run. Regrettably, I couldn't catch up with her."

He shook his head sadly. He had failed his commander.

"Aye, 'tis right sorry I am, Lieutenant. She escaped. A group of militia showed up shortly thereafter to sort out them other two cutthroats I knocked about. They recognized you, sir, and took away them scurvy knaves, leaving us to go peaceably our own way. I brought you straight away back here. I went to the garrison this morning to interrogate the two thugs they caught. They stayed mum about Jemima's possible whereabouts. I've never seen men more scared of a woman than I did them. She's a dangerous one, that's for sure, and those blackguards had no wish to cross her. Aye, other than that, there's nothing more I can tell you, Commander."

"No one blames you, O'Grady. You did the best that you could. Jemima Kaye ought to be on the block for what she did," Robert said. "Put any doubts you have on that matter once and for all to rest. If any finger pointing is to be done, it ought to be directed at me, for my pigheaded impudence in thinking that I could approach her on my own."

He spoke bitterly of his rash behavior, "I behaved like a veritable fool. So full of myself, believing no harm could possibly occur to me. I believed that I was impervious to the same villainous schemes that had struck down Captain Jackson and John Stafford."

He shook his head.

"The only action that can redeem my brash behavior is that I had the intelligence to listen to you, and the crew's advice, in bringing Captain Jackson to Varrik Island. It would appear to be the only intelligent and sane decision I've made thus far."

"Ye mean to say that Captain Jackson is still alive and well, sir?" asked the astonished gunner, looking at Sarah for affirmation.

She nodded. "He's right this moment on the Island of Varrik under my mother's care, recuperating from having been poisoned by Jemima Kaye."

"Poisoned, ye say! Well, I never in me life . . ." the master gunner muttered. "If ever I lay my hands on that vicious harlot—I swear female or not, I'll tear her limb to limb for the harm she's done to our men."

"That is if you can ever lay your hands upon her, Master O'Grady. Undoubtedly, she's by now far away from here and out of the law's reach. It might all be for the best, who knows how many other scurvy rogues she has at her command?" Robert said darkly.

Sarah glanced at him with concern.

She could see that he was taking this disappointment squarely on the chin. He was no longer deluding himself with the possibility of capturing Jemima Kaye. He had been outmaneuvered and outmanned by the cross-dressing hellion.

He frowned, taking a sip of the tea she'd left next to him.

"I must make a full account to the Royal Admiralty on the morrow. They will want to know everything that has happened since I took command. There will be some fuss over my not having alerted them as to Captain Jackson's continued existence. However, I think the events of last night might excuse my obvious omission."

He turned to the gunner. "My memory being what it currently is, I will have to depend on you to fill in the blanks concerning what happened last night. They will probably demand testimony as to what took place at The Hair of The Dog between those ruffians in the alley and us. I'll need your help, O'Grady, in explaining all of this to the Admiralty."

"Aye, aye, sir," the master gunner agreed readily. He understood the seriousness of the matter as the first mate's career was on the line. His future depended upon a favorable review by the naval board.

"I'll try to do my best, sir."

"Good man," said Robert approvingly, his eyes fixed upon the map above him.

It was the same one he had used to chart his first voyage to Varrik Island. Sarah could almost read his thoughts concerning what he intended to do after the Admiral Review Board's inquiry.

"You're planning on returning to Ireland to fetch Captain Jackson back to England, aren't you?" she said. "You've given up pursuing Jemima?"

"Yes, I'll have to leave this matter in the hands of the government for now," he said, resigned. He had no other options open to him.

She knew it was hard for him to swallow his pride and admit defeat. But in his present condition, he could not take on Jemima Kaye and her black-market pirates. He would have to trust the redcoats to try and sniff the possible murderess out. Robert had no other choice. He was physically and mentally beaten. He would have to give up his investigation.

She felt a small measure of his frustration. She too would have liked the assassin captured and punished for her crimes. If not for what happened to Robert last night, then for John Stafford's death and the almost fatal poisoning of Captain Jackson. Aye, such a she-devil ought to be caught and made to pay.

*   *   *

After the master gunner left, she got into bed beside Robert and held him comfortingly in her arms. He turned towards her and started to speak, wanting to tell her how much she meant to him, but she prevented him, placing a finger on his lips.

"*Shush.* . . now is not the time for talking," she said, "For sure now, Robert, I don't want you making any rash promises, which you might later regret. I have no desire to add to your troubles. I want you to promise me you'll wait until we return to my mother's island before we talk about any possible future we might have together. Please, promise me."

Nodding, he agreed.

"Aye, you've the right of it, Sarah. This isn't the time to make life-changing decisions. We don't know how the Admiralty may view the events that have transpired since Captain Jackson took ill and left The Brunswick in my care . . . I may very well find myself walking the docks tomorrow looking for another job, or worse, be clapped in irons."

"Then, let us be together tonight, without any thoughts about tomorrow," she suggested, smiling at him as she laid her head against his chest. "For who knows how much longer we may remain together?"

Agreeing, he lowered his head, capturing her lips with his own. It had been a few days since he'd shaved and she could feel the rough stubble around his lips as he brushed his mouth up against hers.

Gently stroking her face, he looked into her bright blue eyes.

[181]

"Sarah," he said, "You are more than I deserve."

"Am I? Reward me then with that which I desire most," she said, pulling her gown off her shoulders, drawing him closer to her.

"And what would that be?" he asked, smiling, guessing already her reply.

"You, sir, in my bed . . ."

"You are such a demanding woman." He laughed, planting another kiss on her lips, as he helped her remove the remainder of her clothing. "What am I to do?"

"Obey me," she said in a stern manner, imitating him, while holding his manhood in her hands. "And no harm will come to you."

"Indeed, minx," he answered, laughing under his breath as his arousal grew, "I find myself in a vulnerable position. Your orders shall be obeyed to the letter, ma'am. What shall I do next?"

"Make love to me right away, sir."

"Yes, ma'am, willingly, I obey."

He gave her a mock salute, as his other hand moved her underskirts out of his way so that he might access her most intimate of places.

"Hmm . . . ," he said, noticing the knife she kept habitually strapped to her leg. "I doubt very much we shall have need of that tonight. Permission to throw it, ma'am."

"Granted." She laughed, delighted.

He removed it, and with the agility of one used to weapons, adeptly threw it so that it struck the top of the doorframe, where it remained.

"Any other secrets you wish to share with me?" he asked, kissing her neck as his hands reached under her and held her bottom.

"Just this one," she replied, her breath becoming heavy with desire. He placed his firm manhood inside her, their joining was a bittersweet one as their cries echoed throughout the empty ship, for who knew if tomorrow they might not be separated forever. At least tonight they would enjoy and cherish each other.

Chapter 12

The verdict of the Royal Admiralty's Board of Review was quick and swift. Although members of the board expressed displeasure at being kept in the dark about Captain Jackson's true condition, and therefore disapproved of the manner in which the officer was hidden on a tiny island in Ireland, they understood the circumstances of Robert's actions.

It was as one admiral surmised, "Done without any malice towards good Captain Jackson. And as The Brunswick is safely returned here to Portsmouth, we see no reason for Lieutenant Smythe to be reprimanded for doing what he thought was best to protect both Captain Jackson and his crew."

He gave a favorable nod in the young officer's direction.

"Indeed, it is our general opinion that the first mate may have managed to save the same gentleman's life, by bringing him to the learned wise woman . . . and as we have learned, the good Captain Jackson is said to be on the way to what is hoped will be a full recovery of health."

The admiral looked up from the papers from which he was reading the summary of the board's decision. His white wig slipped down a little over his wrinkled brow. He turned a page and continued.

"Now, as to the matter concerning the deserter, ordinary seaman Jeremy Kaye, whom we now know as

Mrs. Jemima Kaye, we have advised that a warrant be issued for her immediate arrest. A reward has been posted for information concerning the murder of Captain Jackson's steward, John Stafford."

He paused in his speech, looking about the room to those who waited on tenterhooks concerning Lieutenant Smythe's future. The hour of reckoning had come.

"As to the attack upon Lieutenant Smythe and that immoral den of iniquity, known as The Hair of The Dog Tavern. . . . Upon the morrow, it is to be permanently closed. It has been deemed an embarrassment to his majesty's navy and a scourge upon our fair land that a den of scoundrels and crooks should be openly operating within the vicinity of this harbor. It shall be immediately closed and torn down."

"We are the center of the Royal British Empire. This sort of evil activity against a naval officer will have serious repercussions. Let it be a warning to other establishments of entertainment that think that we will turn a blind eye to such nefarious activities," said the admiral sternly.

"Huzzah for the Admiralty!" came a shout from among the seamen in the surrounding galleries, interrupting his speech. "Huzzah!"

A large contingent of ex-crewmembers from The Brunswick sat in the public galleries. Many of the seamen had already volunteered to go with a troop of marines to help tear down the disreputable tavern in retribution for what had happened to the well-liked master and commander.

"In conclusion, although we disagree with the secretive manner in which Lieutenant Smythe left Captain Jackson recuperating in Ireland, and the impetuosity in which he pursued his inquiries into the death of John Stafford . . ." The admiral took a moment as he prepared to make his final pronouncement, looking carefully over the parchment in front of him. The gallery held their collective breaths. Would the brave young master and commander receive any undue punishment because of the heinous actions of an evil hellion? Was his promising naval career abruptly to be put to an end? Or was he to be praised and applauded for his unwavering courage and bravery?

"We are, however, pleased with the measures he undertook to safeguard his majesty's frigate, The Brunswick and its crew. He has proven himself an able commander during a tumultuous time. We therefore are unanimous in our decision that acting master and commander, Lieutenant Robert Smythe, shall continue to serve king and country in the Royal Navy. And—" He stopped.

A spontaneous round of applause and cheers broke out. Whistles and catcalls of agreements were heard emitting from the galleries surrounding the courtroom.

The admiral waited until the audience had calmed itself. He then waved a hand for the caterwaul to cease.

He concluded his speech saying, "Upon the safe return of Captain Jackson, further inquiries shall be made as to what rank he shall be rated by his majesty's Admiralty."

"Three cheers for Lieutenant Smythe!" cried out one of the seamen in the gallery.

A round of "Hip, Hip, Hurrahs!" was heard around the chamber, seconding the motion. Hats were thrown in the air and the seamen who had served with Lieutenant Commander Smythe patted each other in joy on the back.

Tears sprung to Sarah's eyes.

The men's open support of Robert brought a most touching and affirmative end to the proceedings. He had been found innocent of any wrongdoings and commended for his bravery. His career as a naval officer would continue as planned. There would be no punishments, only merited commendation.

Robert turned around and gave her a relieved smile. She returned it, watching as seamen and ladies of all ages surrounded him, eager to shake his hand.

Brave and handsome, she knew he would be the talk of the town for days to come. Reporters from the local daily gazettes quickly sketched his profile. The young master and commander had proven himself before the Admiral's Review Board. His record would remain unblemished by the unsavory incidents that surrounded the poisoning of Captain Jackson and the murder of John Stafford.

The recent skirmish with Mrs. Kaye and her cronies at The Hair of The Dog Tavern had reinforced the fact that an evil plot had been afoot, and not successfully executed, aboard the frigate. The sole reason the ship had not gone up in flames was entirely merited to the first mate's ability to lead his crew through a daunting time of terrible crisis.

To what purpose had these unsavory events been planned? It was still unknown.

But Robert knew enough to now be on his guard. For who knew what else Jemima Kaye might have planned for him?

All the dangerous events he had lived through, he silently admitted, had somehow been tied together. There was a common thread. He had but to find it and uncover the whole truth concerning the evil duplicity of Jemima Kaye. He wanted to know why she detested the crew of The Brunswick enough to kill them.

*   *   *

On their way back to the frigate, a tiny woman dressed from head to toe in widow's weeds approached them.

She appeared to be no larger than an overgrown leprechaun.

"Excuse me, ma'am, Lieutenant," she said, clutching a small painted portrait. "Have ye seen this man? He's my husband, Captain James William Fitzpatrick. I'm trying to find out what happened to him and the crew of The Blue Star. Can you help me?"

She held it up to them to inspect.

Looking at the portrait and into the tired face of the lady, Sarah immediately recognized both. "Lady Fitzpatrick!" she exclaimed, acknowledging the eccentric aunt of her dear friend, Lady Beatrice O'Brien.

"Why if it isn't our Wise Sarah!" replied the Irish woman, taking hold of her hands. "I never expected to see you here, m' dear. Faith, what brings ye here to England, lass? And who be this handsome devil of a gentleman beside ye?"

"I'm Lieutenant Robert Smythe, ma'am," he said, stepping forward. He doffed his hat at her in respect. "I am Mistress Duncan's betrothed."

Sarah turned towards him, surprised by his statement. She had not expected him to continue the charade of their engagement after the crew was dismissed . . . unless he wanted to continue their relationship.

She gave him an inquiring look, which said, *What are you up to*? He returned her look with one of his own, a tender one, which caused her heart to skip a beat. It clearly said he wanted to discuss this further in private.

"Ye are!" exclaimed the tiny lady reminding them of her presence, her eyes widening with surprise.

Her gaze ran up and down his handsome frame, comparing him to the deceased rough-and-ready blacksmith the wise woman had once been betrothed to. There was a vast difference between the two.

Where the one had been a large and unrefined peasant

with a quick temper, this gentleman appeared to be the best the English middle class had to offer. He displayed impeccably good manners and had a pleasing way about him. The other had been impetuous and full of unrestrained impulses.

Lady Fitzpatrick's old eyes noted his tarnished gold epaulets. Aye, this young officer was a gentleman who was very sure of himself and undoubtedly knew what he wanted from life.

Standing there in his naval uniform, solicitously taking the time to listen to the tale of woe from an old woman, he reminded Lady Fitzpatrick of someone very dear to her . . . her beloved Captain James Fitzpatrick.

"It is a grand pleasure to make your acquaintance, Lieutenant," she said, smiling up at him, holding her hand out for him to bow over. "I'm Lady Agnes Fitzpatrick.

"And what brings you here to Portsmouth, ma'am?"

"I'm after trying to discover what happened to my husband, Captain Fitzpatrick. I'm hoping to meet someone who can tell me what became of him. He and his ship, the Admiralty says, may have sunk during a storm off the coast of Africa. I am traveling to all the seaports of the known world in hopes of hearing news of him, of running into someone who has either heard or seen him or his ship. But so far, I have been unable to find any. 'Tis as if they disappeared off the face of the earth without a trace to be found."

Lady Fitzpatrick's face crumpled with sad tears.

"They fear all hands were lost in one of the dark uncharted spots off the coast of southern Africa," explained Sarah, picking up the narrative. "It is feared when they were rounding the horn, a squall hit."

She handed a handkerchief to the tearful woman.

"Lady Fitzpatrick has been on this quest for news of her husband and his crew for over three years. She has never given up hope of learning of what became of her good captain and his crew. She has always remained loyal to his memory."

"I cannot go on with my life. I must know what became of my darling husband. I cannot continue . . . ," explained the weeping lady, dabbing at the tears in her eyes.

"Such devotion is indeed most admirable," said Robert, feeling compassion for the grief-stricken widow. "Please, ma'am, won't you join us for a cup of tea? There is a tearoom nearby. It serves the very best kind of refreshments."

"Oh, Lady Fitzpatrick, please do," added Sarah enthusiastically. "It would be an honor for us if you would. We could then sit cozily together like two old village market gossipmongers. And ye could tell me all the latest developments in Urlingford. What has happened between Lady Beatrice and the Earl of Drennan? Last I heard they were betrothed by her father, Lord O'Brien, but she was fighting the match. Ever the Spinster of Brightwood Manor, she was still playing the role of frostbitten maid last I was there."

"My dear, then you truly are behind in the latest!" exclaimed Lady Fitzpatrick, her whole face alit with joy. "My niece and the earl published their banns in church two weeks ago. They are to be married in a fortnight's time in Drennan Castle's chapel. And to everyone's delight, 'tis become a love match made in heaven."

"So true love's course went smoothly for them, after all? They suffered no difficulties?"

"If only it had." The aunt sighed. "There was this terrible business with an old acquaintance of my niece's appearing. The most dreadful man I've ever laid eyes upon. And to think my Beatrice had once almost been married to him! It truly makes one believe that God is watching over us."

The old lady shuddered, recalling the sneering

aristocratic face of the dreadful Viscount Linley. Although born a gentleman of high birth, he had behaved like a cad of the first order.

"When we are seated, I will tell you all. How it came about that this gentleman troubled her and the brave earl. Aye, such a villainous devil as him chills me quite to the bone. Faith, I shall need that cup of tea you offered, after all. For this particular tale requires a bit of time to retell. Are ye certain you're at leisure to hear me out?"

She eyed the couple before her uncertainly.

"Most certainly we have the time. Don't we, Commander Smythe?" asked Sarah, including Robert in the conversation.

She had not missed the admiring glances the old widow cast at Robert. It would be a shame to disappoint her. It was evident she was quite taken with him.

"Indeed, ma'am . . . I shall be most delighted to escort you both to tea." He smiled charmingly, and leading them down Main Street, they walked to a nearby tearoom.

*   *   *

The tearoom was located in the center of the thriving merchant area of Portsmouth. Lace curtains hung in the shop's windows giving it a welcoming feel. It was bustling with activity. The small room was full of women chattering, some of whom were standing at the counter ordering tins of special blends from India, Japan, and China.

Much had changed in the village since Lady Fitzpatrick had lived there as the young wife of a sea captain. It had startled her to see all the fine new structures that had been constructed around the port. The Royal Naval yard, since the war with France, had become an important center of activity for the British Union.

Cupping her tiny hands around a hand-painted piece of fine bone china, Lady Fitzpatrick smiled across at the couple in front of her. Sarah and Robert made a handsome pair. And it had been awhile since she had been among those of close acquaintance who knew her.

"Now, please tell me all the news of Urlingford," said Sarah when a pot of hot brewing Darjeeling tea was placed in front of them. "It has been ever so long since I heard from anyone. I rarely receive any news."

"For sure, I will," said Lady Fitzpatrick.

Briefly, she recounted to them the tale concerning her niece, Lady Beatrice O' Brien's, courtship by the handsome new Earl of Drennan. She ended it by recounting in detail the frightening final battle between the earl and the villainous Viscount Linley, the horrible aristocrat who had hired kidnappers in order to try and force her niece into marriage.

"'I was not there to witness this duel myself, but my brother, Beatrice's father, retold it to me when they came back safely," she said, taking a sip from her dainty cup.

"When I found the dagger that had been left on her bed by those dreadful mercenaries who'd taken my beautiful niece—why, I nearly lost my mind. Aye, it gave me such a terrible fright. To think my Bea' could have ended up at the mercy of that terrible devil . . . it is not to be contemplated."

"I should say not," said Robert.

He himself did not dare to imagine the grief it would cause him if such a thing should happen to Sarah. He had no doubt that he would not hesitate to tear such a cad asunder with his own bare hands.

"I cannot say that I am sorry to have missed the earl skewering that evil man. Nay, I have already had in my own life a fair share of perilous adventures. Faith, wherever I voyaged with my dear James, there was always some new horizon for us to discover together, some small pleasure for us to take in and savor. Aye, I suppose that is what I miss the most, the small delights we shared together in each other's company."

"Were you not lonely at sea with only seamen aboard for company?" asked Sarah, silently wondering what it was like to be an English sea merchant's wife. She was curious as to how the genteel Lady Fitzpatrick had managed to keep herself occupied aboard a small vessel, without all the comforts of a normal home and female companionship.

"Captain Fitzpatrick and I were two of a kind, my dear. Kindred spirits I think is what you would have called us. We were so like minded," said Lady Fitzpatrick, with a small smile, reminiscing. "Aye, he taught me the ways of the sea and how to manage aboard any craft which could float. I learned how to read a sexton and navigate as well as any man. The captain used to teasingly call me his 'able-bodied woman.'"

"Aye, and in time I even came to take pleasure in cooking over a small stove, which had the habit of burning all the undersides of all the dishes I baked." The old woman laughed softly in remembrance. "From the very beginning I loved the sea. And being a captain's wife was as grand a life as any I could have asked God for. Nay, my dears, I have only one regret . . ."

She let out a small sigh, her widow's weeds sagging about her.

"I should have gone with him on that last voyage. It was the only time we were ever separated. Instead, I remained on shore. The captain had wanted me to find us a cozy place to harbor ourselves in our old age. Aye, that last journey was to have been his very last, and sadly it was."

"But you have not given up searching for him?" Sarah asked.

"Nay, I have not. I will one day discover what became of

him, his ship, and The Blue Star's crew. It is only a matter of time. I know that one day my search will come to an end. For all mysteries are solved in due time, are they not?"

"For sure now, my lady, they are," agreed Sarah, meeting the tiny lady's smile with one of her own. She glanced at Robert, who nodded.

It brought back into both their thoughts the mysteries they had yet themselves to solve. Who had killed John Stafford? And why had Jemima Kaye come aboard The Brunswick disguised as a seaman? And what wrong had anyone aboard done to the ex-harlot to invoke such heated hatred?

Looking at Lady Fitzpatrick sipping her tea, Sarah acknowledged she was grateful that she was not faced with the same heartbreaking worry over a lost loved one. She had the comfort of knowing with certainty how John had died. In this she was at peace, unlike the dear lady seated forlornly next to her.

However, what would have happened if those black-hearted thugs had killed Robert before O'Grady showed up? Her heart squeezed at the thought. He could have been tossed into the harbor and disappeared without anyone being the wiser. It was a sobering thought. She easily could have been in Lady Fitzpatrick's shoes.

"Where will you go from here?" she asked, wondering where the tiny lady's wanderings would take her next.

"I intend to return to Urlingford and my brother's home for a few weeks. As I mentioned, Beatrice is finally going to be good and wed. And I want to be there at the tying of the knot."

The widow smiled at her, happily anticipating the approaching nuptials.

"It will be the grandest wedding the parish has seen in many a year. I intend not to miss a minute of it. For sure now, I ought not to be boasting, but I did have a small hand in bringing the two of them together."

"Indeed," murmured Sarah with a matching smile of her own. She could think of several others who had also played their part in this matchmaking, including in a small way, herself and the bride's father.

"Aye, the entire village will be in full celebration over the marriage."

A speculative gleam appeared in the tiny lady's dark green eyes.

"And you and this handsome young officer will attend, won't ye, Sarah?" asked the proud aunt, hedging. The couple before her had that look about them, one that silently suggested they might one day become united in holy matrimony.

Suddenly uncertain, not knowing what the lieutenant thought of their coupling by the wee Irish lady, Sarah did not answer. She couldn't look at him. She hoped he was not displeased by the widow's obvious efforts at matchmaking.

"We'll try to be there," said Robert, smoothly answering for them both.

"Aye, now that would be grand." The lady beamed, nodding. "I know the whole village is awaiting your return, Sarah. You've been sorely missed."

She placed the teacup down and picked up the portrait of her late husband, preparing to take her leave.

"Well, goodbye for now. And God's blessing be upon you both . . . until we meet again. Sarah, take care of yourself."

"And you the same, Lady Fitzpatrick," she murmured back, hoping the old lady would at last find the answers to her questions.

Shaking the lieutenant's hand in a final farewell, refusing his gentlemanly offer to escort her back to the rented cottage where she was staying, the tiny lady disappeared into the hustle and bustle of the street.

Chapter 13

From a distance, Varrik Island looked tranquil in the sunny sea haze. Small white caps topped the water in front of them. Otherwise, a brisk northerly wind blew and the small puncan easily navigated the dark waters.

Sarah was not certain what the future held for her after this day. Robert had become increasingly quiet and thoughtful since the Admiralty's review and he had not spoken at great length with her since their leave taking of The Brunswick. She knew he too was contemplating the future and what it might hold.

She didn't mind the silence between them as they steered the boat towards the island. Looking at Varrik Island off in the distance reminded her of how much she herself had grown since leaving it. The accomplishments she had made allowed her to navigate freely about the world. She had reached all her most cherished goals, except one.

Making a living as a respected village wise woman she no longer needed to hide, to be afraid. She could use her healing abilities where she liked. She had grown into a mature woman of the world, confident in her healing skills. However, there was one thing lacking in her life . . . she had no one to love her, and in her heart she knew she would like to have someone fill that empty space in her life.

Looking up at Robert at the helm, she idly wondered, what it would be like to live with him, to be a permanent part of his life. Would they rub together as well as they did now?

This was a dream she had dared not to think upon. It was one she knew was becoming more and more desirable. It had been a long time since she had dreamt of sharing her life with anyone.

Robert adjusted the sail. The sun lit his dark locks, giving a warm glow to his appearance. Despite the marring of his face from the alley beating, he looked manly and confident. From habit she turned the ring on her finger. Looking down at the small gold heart held by two hands, she pondered her own heart's desires.

Aye, I could fall in love and have a family if I want. There was nothing, not even the cherished memory of a dead love to prevent me. It's my decision. But do I dare? Am I ready to leave my secure position as the respected wise woman of Urlingford village, for the more precarious one as an English naval officer's lady? Should I abandon all I've worked so hard for in order to follow my heart's leading?

She knew the fork in the road lay ahead. They would either continue to grow closer and plan a future together as a couple, or be separated, possibly forever.

The thought of never seeing him again caused a small tug of fear in her heart. She pressed her hand to it. She knew what she wanted. She would have to tell him soon how she felt.

When they arrived upon the pebbled beach of Varrik Island, Gladys Clogheen and Captain Jackson made their appearance, carrying a wicker basket full of crabs between them. They had just returned from checking Gladys's pots. A small quarter boat moored nearby. Captain Jackson waved a hand at them and smiled by way of greeting.

Robert surveyed his friend and commander, surprised by the changes in him. The deathly ill man he'd left in the care of Sarah's mother looked miraculously almost like his former self.

Captain Jackson's pale hollow cheeks were now flush again with the ruddy vigor of good health. His body had filled out. His skin no longer sagged on his bones. Although still thin from the poisoning, he could tell that the senior officer would soon be hearty and whole again. There was no doubt the good captain had shaken off the specter of death.

"Here, Gladys, let me get this for you," said the senior officer, carrying the heavy basket to the waiting handcart partly filled with driftwood. "Now why are ye standing there gaping at me for, Smythe?"

"I—I just can't quite believe my eyes, sir," he stuttered.

He turned to Gladys and said honestly, "It is a veritable miracle you've performed on Captain Jackson, ma'am."

"What me?" The wise woman laughed. "I had no hand in it, Lieutenant. 'Tis the commander here himself who refused t' roll over into his grave."

She shook a finger at the captain's turned back.

"Nay, sir, he's about as pigheaded as one of my island goats sitting in a patch of turnips. Stubborn is that man . . . aye, he's too obstinate to let death take him. I've no doubt he'll wrestle Saint Peter himself on the momentous day he opens the pearly gates for him. But as ye can see, that'll not be anytime soon."

Sarah blinked at her mother's girlish laughter. It was a sound she'd not heard in a long time. She secretly was taken aback by the compliments her mother paid Captain Jackson.

What had happened? What common ground had those two found to base their existing friendship upon?

And what had been the most unexpected surprise was the change of attitude in her mother. Usually,

Gladys moaned aloud over how foolish her patients were. This positive report was indeed most unexpected.

Had Captain Jackson somehow managed to break down her mother's aloof wall? How had he won over Gladys's cautious distrust of men? She gave her mother a sly glance. She wanted to ask what had occurred while she was gone.

In turn, noticing the odd inquiring look, Gladys responded, "Darling gel, I'm not going to tell you, so, don't ask. For sure now, 'tis none of your concern, now is it? 'Tis between him and I what happened here while you were gone."

"Hmm . . . for sure," was Sarah's prim reply. She was not overly concerned. Her usually reticent mother had never been one to rush into anything.

She wisely decided that if her mother and the good Captain Jackson had developed some sort of friendship, then splendid. Her mother had been alone on this remote island for a long time. She deserved some companionship. And if the good Captain Jackson was the one to finally provide it, well then, God bless him.

She had always said she wanted her mother to have a friend her own age. And now she had one, an English officer who was going to return to his people. That fact stung a little. It had not been her own often spoken concern that had brought about this change, but the presence of an outsider.

Perhaps now I can convince Mother to come and live with me? To finally convince her to leave this tiny island. She thought optimistically of this unexpected turn of events.

Her mother was inching towards fifty. She wasn't young anymore. And the island could be a dangerous place to live on alone. One good typhoon and both her mother and the cottage could be swept clean off the island hill.

But as she watched her mother bend to pick up strands of seaweed off the beach to mulch her garden with, she secretly doubted she could convince Gladys to leave. She looked at Captain Jackson and wondered if perhaps he could. She had never given any thought to the possibility that a man, especially an officer such as Captain Jackson, might befriend her mother.

Perhaps he was the one to persuade her mother to leave? If she wouldn't do it for her, maybe she would for him.

Robert helped pull the handcart up the island's hill. Captain Jackson manned the other side. The two men panted as they maneuvered it upward.

"Hard to port, Lieutenant," the older man muttered, steering clear of a large puddle.

Goats bleated in greeting as they passed. Gladys stopped and patted one of the baby kids on the head, calling it by name. The little goat, trustingly, let her pet it.

Aye, thought again Sarah, watching, *it's going to be difficult to persuade her to come away with us. This is her home. She's always been happy here.*

*   *   *

Supper that night comprised of steamed mussels, clams, and fish caught that day by boat. Added to this were potatoes pulled from the vegetable garden behind the cottage. They sat companionably about a large wooden trestle table eating, sharing tales about what had passed since they last saw one another.

When Robert came to the part about Jemima's deception and how she and her men had attacked him at The Hair of The Dog, Captain Jackson commented, "'Tis good that you forced her to show her true colors. You've done well, Robert."

Jackson puffed thoughtfully on a clay dhudeen pipe. A cloud of smoke ringed about him. He pointed the end of the pipe in his direction.

"I'll stand by you when the Admiralty interviews me about what happened. Never fear, there's naught to worry. I hold myself accountable for letting that poisonous Lucrezia Borgia aboard The Brunswick. And you say, like that Italian she-devil, she and her men attacked you? Why the sharp fanged barracuda. Sharpen her teeth on you, did she?"

Robert looked shamefacedly down at the turf fire. He said nothing, his expression as dark as his thoughts. He blamed himself for everything. He should have been more alert, ready for any and all dangers.

Jackson took note of this and laid a comforting hand on the younger officer's shoulder. "Don't take it so hard, Smythe. There is naught that you could have done. 'Tis best you rest and clear your thoughts of all blame. On the morrow we'll leave for England and I'll clear up any troubles that might remain from my resurrection. I imagine there were one or two who were astounded to learn of my true fate."

"Aye, it was if they heard of Lazarus's rising from the dead, sir," agreed Robert.

That, thought Sarah, was an understatement.

She had witnessed firsthand the winsome Fiona Foxworthy faint into Second Lieutenant Litton's arms when it was announced. She had been the one to hand a small silver vial of smelling salts to him to administer beneath the vixen's upturned dainty nose.

Speculative glances had been cast in her direction by several members of the crew upon hearing the news. Some of the officers had smiled warmly at Sarah, hoping the betrothal between her and the master commander was now officially called off. Robert had taken her hand, ending any doubts concerning the validity of their relationship. They had become a couple. He was not about to relinquish her to another.

She looked up from the stack of dishes she had been gathering in preparation of cleaning them by the well. The time to talk to him about their future together was fast approaching. As much as she was eager to go forward with her life, she was equally afraid of what he might decide. Perhaps his career in the Royal Navy would exclude him from having an Irish wise woman for a wife? And if so, then this would be the end of their relationship and a final goodbye between them.

Thoughtfully, she left the cottage carrying the dishes in front of her. She never made it to the well. A pair of rough hands grabbed her from behind.

She felt the sharp prick of a knife at her back.

"'Don't breathe a word," said a nervous, twitchy male voice behind her. "I swear I'll-I'll hurt you if you don't do what I say. I-I swear it."

Sarah slowly turned and eyed the man who had been standing behind her.

He was almost the same height as she. His features reminded her of a thin, nervous weasel she'd once spied catching fish at a local pond. He was ready to take flight at the slightest sign of trouble.

She came to a swift decision. Lifting the dishes up, she swiftly brought the entire pile soundly down upon the brigand's head.

Crack!

He immediately collapsed in front of her.

After kicking him gently with her wood clog, she took a deep breath and screamed. But no help came from the cottage. Instead, out of the shadow of a nearby tree stepped the person she least in the world desired to see—Jemima Kaye.

The cross dressing she-devil stood before her in a gentleman's, long silk coat. Her shapely legs were clothed in the same dark leather breeches she'd worn as Jeremy, aboard The Brunswick. A long gypsy scarf held her wiry hair back. Two gold hoop earrings dangled from each ear. Dark eyes flashed menacingly like daggers in her direction.

"What do you want?" Sarah asked. Her fear almost caused her to choke on the words. She could tell by the dangerous look in Jemima's eyes why she had come. But she could not help but ask the question. "Why did you come here?" She wanted a response, even if it was her executioner announcing her death sentence. She wanted the extra time it might provide for her to think of a way to escape. She had to think of a way to get away from her.

"I've come to finish the job I started. I've come to finish you off," said the pirate evenly, advancing on her with a cocked blunderbuss in one hand and a long sword in the other. "This way I make certain that none of you survive."

"Well, ye can't have me," said Sarah frantically picking up some of the broken plates she had dropped.

She madly threw them at Jemima, ignoring the small cuts she made into the palm of her hands as she threw them. Her thoughts were only of protecting herself. One sharp piece of broken pottery grazed Jemima's cheek. The pirate raised her gun hand to protect herself against Sarah's assault. It appeared she wanted to be at close range when she killed her.

"You can't stop me," Jemima said, taking one step closer. "No one can."

"Aye, is that so? Well then, I'll be damned if I don't try, won't I?" she retorted, taking a few short steps backwards.

Sarah's gaze traveled up the hill to the cottage. Where was Robert? Why hadn't he come to her rescue? Hadn't anyone heard her scream?

A few cracking shots of gunpowder were heard from

the cottage's direction. Dear heavens, the others were being attacked, just as Jemima said! They could not come and help her. They were trapped in the cottage. She would have to find a way to survive, using her wits. No one was coming to rescue her.

Her hand reached out and felt something cold and solid behind her.

She was standing in the narrowest part of the trail leading down to the beach. A large boulder now stood between her and what existed on its other side, air and sea. She reached out to it, hoping to anchor herself.

Terrified, she hugged the boulder.

Slowly, she edged around its cold surface, putting it between herself and Jemima. She was mindful she was one step away from the cliff and a sheer drop into the sea below.

If only I could run past Jemima, she thought frantically, looking for an escape route. *Then I could hurry down the other side of the hill to the cove and summon help from a passing fishing vessel.*

Jemima, however, would not let her break away. The instant she tried to run, the hellion leapt forward, grabbing the sleeve of Sarah's gown.

The lace ripped.

Sarah tried to yank away the thin material from the outreaching hands of the harlot.

Holding up her blunderbuss, Jemima aimed it at Sarah's face.

"You think your precious lieutenant will come and save you?" She sneered, dragging her forcefully to the edge. "Give him no more thought or tears, my dear. He's dead . . . I ordered my men to kill him on sight. He can no more save you than I could save my own dear husband."

Dead? Sarah couldn't believe it. She wouldn't believe it. *No! Not Robert.*

"What does your husband's death have to do with this?" Sarah asked instead, her teeth chattering. She was frightened and she needed time to think. She could see the edge of the cliff. "Why do you hate the members of The Brunswick so much? Why do you want all of us dead?"

"That's right . . . ye still don't know, do you? Captain Edward Kaye, my husband, was the captain of La Belle Chance. The black-market runner The Brunswick captured. And when Captain Jackson and your precious Lieutenant Smythe took his ship, they caused his death."

"But how was he murdered?"

"As good as . . . La Belle Chance was smuggling French silk and other goods into England. That is until The Brunswick captured her. My husband was trapped. His men told me that he fought like a wounded bear until the end. Then, when he realized all was lost, rather than be made a prisoner to sit in some stinking English jail, he chose to blow his brains out."

"Robert and Captain Jackson did not kill him. He put an end to his cursed life with his own hands," exclaimed Sarah, knowing she was trying to reason with a mad woman. "And yet you continue to blame them. Revenge won't bring back your husband. It will only bring you more pain once the militia catches up with you."

"That's a risk I'm willing to take!" Jemima glared angrily at her. She spat at the ground, cursing all English.

"If The Brunswick had not captured his ship, my husband would be alive today . . . and now I want a widow's revenge, and you, ye Irish witch, shall provide it!"

She advanced on her. The ivory handle holding the sharp blade gleamed in the pale moonlight. She grabbed her, placing its sharp tip up against her pale throat.

Sarah winced. She felt a sharp prick on her skin. A trickle of blood dripped down her neck. She gritted her teeth.

She was alone. No one was coming. She had to think of a way out.

"I understand what it's like to be alone," she said, desperately trying to appeal to Jemima's sense of humanity, whatever there was left to appeal to. "I was abandoned as a baby and brought up by a woman many considered to be a witch. We were chased away by foolish villagers to this remote place. However, I found happiness and peace despite all of that and then eventually I left here to forge a new life for myself on the mainland."

"You can do the same. You can leave here and start over. You don't have to do this. You can go to Barbados or Spain and start fresh somewhere else. You can be happy." For a moment, silence reigned between them as Jemima mulled over her words. She could see some of the murderous gleam in her eyes die. She needed to get her talking.

"Why did you kill the steward, Stafford?" she asked, knowing he had joined the crew after the capture. "What did he have to do with your husband's death? He was innocent of any wrongdoing."

"I had to kill him. He saw me set fire to the mizzenmast with the torch I'd made. He tried to stop me. Don't you see, ye daft girl . . . I had to get rid of him."

Jemima eyed her crazily.

"We fought, and he managed to knock me down. He was getting up to call for help . . . I stood up and stabbed him, throwing his lifeless body overboard. His cursed ghost came back and haunted me, pointing his accusing finger. You saw him. I had to take flight or be damned. No one knew I'd killed him."

"But you're wrong. Stafford's body was found, and

pulled from the sea with your knife still in him. He was laid to rest in peace by a priest, his spirit set free."

"If I could have, I would've destroyed them all. They all deserved to die for what they did to my poor husband!"

She laughed madly, her voice full of hatred, tears falling unchecked down her cheeks, as she gulped them back. "The entire crew played a part in my beloved Edward's death. They all deserved to die. And now it's your turn."

Sarah felt the edge of the cliff through her slippers. In another minute she would be over. Looking down at the sea made her dizzy. She felt her body pitch forward slightly.

Panic overtook calm reasoning. Without any thought as to the consequences, she grabbed frantically at Jemima's wrist.

Her only sane thought was to get as far away as possible from the edge. Using all her weight, Sarah tried to pull herself away from the cliff. But at that moment, unknowingly, she catapulted both herself and the mad woman over the edge, both screaming in terror as they fell into nothing.

Sarah landed on the sloping side of the rocky cliff. Her body rolled a little towards the sea. Jemima's body dropped clear into free air. When her body hit the earth again, it smashed upon an outcropping of jagged island rocks.

Within minutes a white-foamed wave swelled up from the sea's depths and swept the dead woman away. Not a sign of her remained, but a floating red gypsy scarf.

Dirt and shrub bit into Sarah's skin as she slipped downwards.

Frantically, she tried to stop herself. She reached out, grabbing at shrubs and rock, until at last she caught

[207]

a branch. Her left foot lodged into a protruding rock. She hung precariously onto the thin evergreen with both hands, closing her eyes against the vertigo. The world around her tilted uncontrollably. She squeezed her eyes shut.

Below she could hear the pounding of the sea's surf as it rushed up against the island's rocks. The sea's spray almost touched her feet. If she let go now, she too would be swept away into the sea and drowned.

She hung there, praying that somehow she would be found. Hoping against hope, she prayed she would survive and outlive this nightmare.

It seemed like an eternity and then she heard something.

Voices from above cried out, "Sarah! Sarah! Where are you?"

"I'm here. I'm here . . . below you!" she yelled up.

She willed herself to remain calm, clinging to the small branch. She wasn't going to grant that black-hearted she-devil her last wish.

"There's no reason to be afraid . . . I'm alive . . . I'm alive," she repeated to herself, calming her heart. "And they've found me!"

She heard the sound of something being thrown down from the cliff's edge above her. Small rocks pebbled her face. Suddenly, it was calm.

She peeked to her right. A ladder rope was now dangling down next to her.

It was the same kind she had seen Robert use to climb up the side of The Brunswick's sides. Her heart surged with hope. Maybe Jemima had lied. Perhaps the murderess had said Robert was dead in order to try and diminish her will to live.

Oh, please, dear Lord, she prayed fervently, *let him be alive. Please let him be alive . . . I love him so much . . . I want to have a life with him.*

Waiting, she closed her eyes, willing herself to be strong.

She listened as someone climbed down to her. More pebbles rained down on her face and arms. Some brave soul was coming down to get her. She was not going to be forced to act alone. Someone was risking his own life to help rescue her.

"Sarah," said the familiar voice she had over the past month grown to cherish. "I'm here, my love . . . give me your hand. I'll put you onto the ladder next to me."

She held out her hand and felt Robert's hand firmly grip hers. However, unable to resist the urge, she glanced downward. Her world tilted out of control.

Frightened, she released her hold.

"Don't let go!" he urged.

He caught her wrist and placed her hand onto the ladder. She closed her eyes, dread hitting the center of her stomach. She wanted to be sick. She wanted to be anywhere but here. She wanted to magically disappear off this cliff. She wanted to be a bird and fly away.

The only real feeling that bound her to earth was the tight grip of his hand over hers, his voice urging her to hold on, to not give-up. He held onto the ladder with effortless strength. He acted as one who had spent years in the highest top yards and crows nests of three masted warships. His strong left arm pulled her up beside him.

His body acted as a solid wall upon which she could depend to keep her safe, protecting her from falling. She leaned into the rope. She was not going to give in to the vertigo.

"Hello, Sarah," he whispered comfortingly into her ear. "I'm right here, darling."

She took a deep breath. Her eyes remained firmly shut.

No, I'm not going to faint. I'm going to get myself back to where I belong. I can do this. I can get up there.

She felt him place both of her hands on the ropes.

"It's going to be all right," he said, his voice sounding tender. "We're going to get you out of here. Don't let go."

She felt his firm arms go about her. He had positioned himself a little beneath and behind her. His strong arms wrapped themselves around her waist. His body acted as a protective shield from the sheer drop below him.

Swallowing the lump of fear in her throat, she asked, "How are we going to do this?"

"One step at a time. One step at a time. Hands, and then feet. Until we reach the top. And I'll be with you the entire time. I won't let you fall, love."

And that was exactly what they did. Slowly, rung-by-rung, they went up together. They acted as if they were one. Carefully, they climbed to the rim of the cliff above. Hand over hand, one foot at a time, always looking up, never down.

With only five rungs remaining, Sarah saw dark green tufts of grass hanging over the cliff's edge. Several sturdy seamen reached down. They pulled her up.

Her feet once again touched solid ground. She had not granted that mad woman's vengeful wish. She had managed to survive.

She looked about her, dazed, seeking out familiar sights and sounds. The grass beneath her had never looked so wonderfully green before.

Upon spying her mother's face, they both let out cries of joy.

Gladys hurried to her daughter's side, tears streaming down her face. The long, comfy wrap she wore flapped in the wind like a beautiful black bird.

She held onto her beloved child, murmuring, "Thank the good Lord above that you are truly alive and well.

All the saints above answered my prayers for your lives to be spared."

Upon learning that Jemima Kaye had gone to a watery grave, the older woman growled, "Got what she deserved, did she . . . well then, I hope to high heavens that Lucifer has her hopping madly about on the brimstone. Aye, that dark sea witch's soul no doubt is with him now. For sure when the angel of death comes it does not go away empty handed, does it?"

"Her heart was broken, Mother. She went insane with grief, refusing to let herself be healed. I tried to convince her."

Tears gleamed in her eyes at her remembrance of the dangerous encounter.

"Shush now . . . don't upset yourself any further. There was nothing you could have done," murmured her mother comfortingly. She lovingly brushed back a strand of her daughter's golden hair.

"Sometimes, darlin', we can't help the broken ones."

She nodded, silently agreeing with her mother. Jemima had chosen her own destiny. There was nothing she could have said or done to change the fate of the other woman.

Robert, brushing off his clothes, heaved a sigh of relief. Captain Jackson heartily thumped him on the back in delighted greeting. Several fishermen warmly pressed his hand.

The local fishermen had been passing by Varrik Isle when they heard the same gunshots as Sarah. Upon spying the pirate ship anchored nearby, they'd rightly concluded that the famous wise woman and her daughter were in trouble.

The courageous fishermen had abandoned their nets, deciding to rout the pirates off the tiny island. The blockade runners, upon being surrounded by the armed and angry sons of Erin, scurried off like frightened bilge rats to safer waters.

A look passed between Sarah and Robert, one that she would remember for the rest of her life. Her mother gently released her. She too had noticed their unspoken bond.

Robert gazed down at the small ring she wore. He gently turned it around. "I've been told that when a married woman wears this on her left hand, it means something about two hearts becoming one."

"Aye," she answered, her blue eyes meeting his. "It means two loves have been joined."

"And so it is . . ." He nodded, kissing her cheek. "Sarah, will you do me the honor of becoming forever a part of my heart, never to leave my side?"

He took her hand in his.

"What I'm humbly asking you is . . . will you become my lady and be mine for as long as I breathe?" he asked. "I cannot see my life without you in it, Sarah. You are the bravest, most beautiful woman I've ever known, Please, will you have me?"

"Oh . . . aye," she answered joyfully.

She raised her face to his and kissed him in a tender, passionate kiss, pledging herself to him. The sound of the sea behind them crashed against the rocks as the sun slowly sank in the horizon. They stood together bathed in the glow of pale hazy light. The ruby stone set in the middle of the ring glowed.

Two hearts had found each other. Two hearts had been joined, never to part. They would truly have a wonderful life together. The captain and his lady. It was meant to be. Sarah cried tears of joy. They were alive and in love. She would travel with him, wherever the winds took them. She would be by his side, helping him in any way she could, his true-life partner and love.

Author's Biography

Engaging, romantic frolics are how author, Beverly Adam, describes her Regency Romance series: *Gentlemen of Honor*. The redheaded writer currently resides in California where she revisits history on a regular basis as a romance novelist and biographer.